D1189895

INFINITE DIMENSIONS

Also by Jessica Treadway

INFINITE DIMENSIONS

STORIES

BY

JESSICA TREADWAY

DELPHINIUM BOOKS

INFINITE DIMENSIONS

For information, address DELPHINIUM BOOKS, INC.,
16350 Ventura Boulevard, Suite D
PO Box 803
Encino, CA 91436

Library of Congress Cataloguing-in-Publication Data is available
on request.
ISBN 978-1-953002-11-2
22 23 24 25 LSC 10 9 8 7 6 5 4 3 2 1

First Edition

Jacket and interior design by Colin Dockrill

To Ann Olson Treadway, who read me my first stories,
and to Phil Holland, love true

CONTENTS

KWASHIORKOR

These days she moved through the world with the sense that she had either escaped from prison or been set free. The relief never left her; no matter what she did or thought about, it ran beneath, a current of euphoria at finding herself on the other side of captivity. A dozen moments a day, she felt shocked by her own happiness. It kept revealing itself to her, a surprise each time. She had not since she was a child been tempted to believe in God, but she considered it now because she so often felt the impulse to thank someone—or something—for the tectonic shift that had sealed shut the fault lying under her life.

What the fault consisted of exactly, she did not know. She had not discerned it in all the years with so many therapists, or during the hospital stays she endured when her condition paralyzed her to the point that she could not keep herself safe, to use the therapists' term.

Act as if, the last one had counseled her, when Amy said she didn't feel worthy of having the kind of life that seemed to come so naturally to everyone else. *Pretend you're the person you want to be. They've done studies. You'll start to feel that way.* Amy scoffed at this New Age hooey—weren't they supposed to uncover, together, what lay at the heart of her despair?—but she must have followed the advice without being conscious of doing so, and it had worked.

Her husband, Jack, said it was all to her credit, that she alone had pulled herself out of what he referred to as her "bad time," which he had never witnessed. Amy herself was sure that the only thing separating her from the dead patients was luck. She certainly wasn't a better person than those who never recovered themselves; in fact, she suspected she was worse. Though once it happened—the correction, the conversion—she resolved to do her best to believe she deserved this better life, and to live up to the kind of person she seemed to have become.

The truth was that she rarely let herself think about the woman she had been before she married Jack, before they became parents to Laurel, before they moved to the town she'd once driven to three days a week for her appointments with the psychiatrist Amy could barely bring herself to look at because the other woman was so clearly superior to her in every way that just meeting her eyes caused her to choke with humiliation. She seldom let herself remember details from her stays in the hospital, such as eating meals with plastic forks because she couldn't be trusted with stainless, or the pride she felt when she worked her way up to the privilege of going to sleep without a "sitter" assigned to watch her all night from a chair by the rubbery bed.

She knew that she probably should have figured out, by now, what it was that accounted for her transformation from a psychiatric patient on suicide watch to someone who managed other people's money for a living, not to mention an attorney's wife and a soccer mom. Soccer mom! As ridiculous a status as she knew it was to aspire to, when she sat on the sidelines to watch Laurel play with the other kids in the Hobbit League, she had the distinct feeling that this, *this*, was what clinched it—she was normal now, there was no going back. She didn't let herself think about the time she'd tucked her hair up into a baseball cap, then pulled the cap down over her eyes, before sneaking into these same bleachers to watch her therapist's son playing offense for his team. She'd watched the therapist chatting and laughing with the other mothers, feeling her own failure grow and gather in her gut. By the time she left the field, she was doubled over. She never told the therapist what she'd done, and—improbably, inexplicably—it was soon after this episode that she began waking in the mornings feeling lighter than she could remember, pods of hope pinging in her heart.

A fluke, she thought. At least at first. But when the hope persisted—when she felt stronger, and the strength kept building on itself, multiplying, pitching her forward into a life more joyful than she had ever dared to imagine, she made the decision without quite realizing it to forget about all those years, or at least to push them so far aside that they rarely if ever intruded on her now.

She also understood in some unvisited cellar of herself that by not understanding why her unhappiness left her, she might be inviting it to come back.

It had not returned, so far. But Dina Broward had.

Amy recognized her immediately. She hadn't bothered to look at the résumé beforehand, and her punishment was a mouthful of metal verging on vomit as she reached out to shake hands. That cap of dark hair, the face with its flat features that looked as if the manufacturer hadn't quite bothered to punch them fully out of the mold—there it all was before her, shrinking within the short, almost indented figure whose default stance was one of apology. It took Dina a few more moments, but by the end of the greeting she'd put it together, Amy saw. "Oh," Dina said, having to reach behind her to locate the seat before she lowered herself into it, across from Amy's desk. "Oh, God. Goodness. You're the last person I expected to see. I mean, in this situation." She thumped her chest with a fist in the gesture Amy remembered, as if dislodging something that had come to rest uncomfortably inside. "How—how are you?" She leaned across the desk, then pulled back when she realized (Amy could read it in her face) that it was not an appropriate question for a job applicant to ask the interviewer.

Dina's unease made it possible for Amy to act benevolent, even serene. "I'm fine," she said, reminding herself without using the exact words in her mind that she held the power now, and that if she tried hard enough, she might be able to erase from Dina's mind (as she had almost erased from her own) the images from their time together on the women's unit at Goddard Hospital, ten years earlier, after Amy had been transported there by police who'd been called when the security guard at her place of employment—she worked as a receptionist for a law firm—found her climbing up and down the three flights of stairs comprising the firm's floors, after hours (*long* after hours; it was two a.m.), and couldn't get her to stop. She'd explained to them that she was only trying to exhaust herself because she couldn't sleep, hadn't slept in ages, and there must have been some other reason, too, that they took her to the hospital instead of home, because just climbing stairs didn't seem like enough to get yourself committed, but she never asked and so she never found out, but that was okay because she didn't really care to.

At the hospital she was given something that put her to sleep, and she could not have felt more grateful for those hours of blank peace. The next morning they moved her in with Dina, whose favorite thing to do was stand in front of the corkboard above her bureau and look at the photographs she had arranged there. Famine. Funerals. Bombings. Stampedes. They wouldn't let her use thumbtacks because of the sharp points, but one of the nurses had supplied a pad of yellow sticky notes that held the photos in place. Occasionally one came undone and fell to the bureau, and Dina drew in her breath as if trying not to panic, breathing heavily through her nose as she hurried to replace the sticky and press it more firmly into the board.

The pictures, clipped carefully from magazines and newspapers, depicted an assortment of suffering. Dina said they made her feel better because they reminded her of all the people who were worse off than she. They gave her perspective, she said. The doctors on the unit were of two minds about the display. One supported it because he said it provided relief to Dina, a distraction from the spinning loop of destructive thoughts that plagued her every moment she was awake. The other doctor believed the pictures should be taken down because they only perpetuated that loop. In the end they compromised: She could tape the photographs up to the board every morning, and spend as much of her unassigned time looking at them as she wished, but after lunch she had to take them down and turn them in to the nursing station, where they would be held until after breakfast the next day. Dina agreed, but Amy understood that it was only because she knew she had no other choice.

Her second day on the unit, she walked by as Dina was removing a photo captioned "Kwashiorkor." Amy leaned forward to sound out the word under the picture of the African child whose face was swollen but whose bones were visible through his skin. Kwashiorkor, Dina told her, was a disease caused by lack of protein. "I like it because it's a beautiful word for something ugly," she said. "I like things like that." The word came from Ghanaian for "dethroned," because the first children diagnosed with it had been replaced at their mothers' breasts too soon by subsequent children, who deprived their older siblings of what they still needed, causing those siblings to grow sick. In group therapy later that day, Amy would learn that Dina had a special sensitivity to this circumstance: she herself had been an unexpected, hidden twin, not known to exist until her sister had been pulled from their mother's body. Even then, it was only an observant nurse who noticed there was another baby inside; the first twin had sucked up most of the nutrients, leaving Dina the dregs. She weighed a little more than two pounds and spent her whole life trying to catch up. As an adult who had never learned to drive or earned a degree, lived on her own or understood how to talk to strangers, she believed it was because she hadn't received enough oxygen, in the womb, that she'd never developed these skills. One of the other women in group said, "Bullshit, you just like being a victim," but the doctor shushed her and told Dina he understood why she felt that way.

Amy and Dina shared that room in the corner of the women's unit for twenty-seven days, until Dina's state insurance ran out and she went to live with an aunt who offered her room and board in exchange for chores and Dina's monthly disability check. Amy said they should exchange phone numbers so they could call each other when they needed to, and remain friends "out there." Dina gave the crooked smile indicating she believed she knew better, but she scribbled her number on a yellow sticky and pressed it to the bureau between their beds.

The next morning, Amy woke up to find they had moved someone else in with her, an anorexic sixty-year-old who chewed her sheets in her sleep. Only then did Amy appreciate how much Dina had meant to her. They hadn't just been randomly assigned roommates in a hospital; they had come to know and recognize each other like dying people, or like two people in love. Much of it happened through whispered conversations at night during the half-hour intervals between the nurses' flashlight bed-checks, when everyone on the unit knew enough to close their eyes and pretend to be asleep.

And they had laughed. Amy knew most people would not expect psychiatric patients to have such keen senses of humor, let alone anything to laugh about. But if humor involved reducing things to their essence, what better place to locate the essential than in a hospital for the most sad? Were you dead or were you alive—that's what it came down to. Dead, not so funny. But the realm of *alive* gave you so much room to play with, along with a giddiness that came only from knowing how bad things could have been, but weren't, at least not right then.

On the thirtieth day, Amy signed herself out. She'd convinced the doctors that she was better, and convinced herself, too. She graduated from the hospital's constant care to the three-times-a-week sessions, then two, then one, with the therapist who was the mother of the soccer-playing son. Shortly after that, she met Jack and got the position as assistant branch manager in her therapist's town. She threw away the sticky containing the phone number she'd never called, and began moving through the world with the sense that she had either escaped from prison or been set free.

And now here came Dina Broward, looking for a job. Grateful to be able to gaze down at her desk for as long as she might need, Amy read her old roommate's résumé and couldn't help feeling impressed and a little proud. Dina had pulled herself together and gone back to school, then worked at a bank in an entry position for two years before being promoted to customer liaison. With Amy she was interviewing for a job at the next level, account representative.

"It wouldn't be too stressful?" Amy said, not exactly intending to put the idea into Dina's mind. But she did not want to see this woman every day. She wanted the opposite, to flick Dina Broward back to where she came from. Start this morning over in the now familiar luxury of forgetting that she'd inhabited that space, too, and lived in dread of returning, no matter how much she tried to pretend otherwise.

She could tell they both recognized her question as one she would not have asked of anyone else. Dina stood and began to collect her belongings. "This is totally awkward; I get that. But I promise, I had no idea I was coming to see *you.*" Her tone turned just the slightest bit defensive. "You have a different last name."

"I got married." Amy shrugged a little, feeling the need to apologize; surely marriage was a life development Dina could still only imagine for herself.

"Anyway, I don't expect you to hire me. I understand it's too weird." Dina was standing now, though Amy had not risen to join her. "If I were in your shoes, I wouldn't do it."

Later, Amy would wonder exactly how calculating Dina had been in making this last remark. They both knew what she said wasn't true; they both knew that in the same position, Dina would not hesitate to offer her old friend the job, no matter how much trepidation she felt at doing so.

Not wanting to appear any less generous, Amy stood and held out her hand, and Dina paused in bewilderment before shaking it. "I'm glad to see you again, Dina," Amy said, hoping to convey a warmth that didn't look as constructed as it felt. "I'll recommend you to the manager for the position—you should fit in just fine."

The time to have told Jack about her encounter with Dina, and the apprehension it raised in her, was that night. But something held her back from saying anything as they sat with their decaf after dinner, and after that it felt too late. Giving Laurel her bath, Amy tried to wash her daughter's hair with the bottle of body soap instead of shampoo, and Laurel shrieked and laughed, thinking her mother was playing a joke; of course Amy pretended this had been her plan all along.

After the branch manager approved Dina based on Amy's recommendation, Amy assigned Dina to Trevor for training, without acknowledging to herself the secret hope that his ornery, impatient nature would scare off the new employee, create enough anxiety in her that she'd feel compelled to quit. She hadn't counted on the rapport that seemed to spring up between them almost immediately; later on that first day, Trevor told Amy she'd made a great hire, Dina was a quick study, she'd work out well. Amy stammered "Great" through her falsest smile.

Dina made friends fast. Two days during that first week, she brought her lunch and ate it in the employees' room (or, as the weather was unusually warm for September, on the bench in front of the bank), but on the other three days she went out for sandwiches with Trevor or one of the tellers. Amy recognized what they all saw in her. She remembered it—a paradoxical mix of vulnerability and the distinct sense she exuded that she had been through the worst already and could not be hurt. It intrigued people, made them wish they could feel the same way.

Sealing the deal was her standby, her parlor trick: she could almost always recite for people, when she met them, the meaning of their first names. Trevor was *industrious*; the tellers, Jada and Katherine, were *wise* and *pure*. In the hospital Dina had told Amy that her name meant *beloved*, which Amy hadn't heard before. She held on to this, and years later, when Jack proposed and said that he knew her name meant *beloved* and he was here to tell her she was, she took it as a sign. So it could be said that Dina had been a kind of midwife helping her give birth to this life she had now, though by then they'd long lost touch and Amy had no intention of reconnecting for the purpose of describing the coincidence or expressing gratitude.

On her first payday, Dina stopped by Amy's office door and said timidly, "You wouldn't want to go to lunch, would you? My treat? I wouldn't have this job if it weren't for you."

There it was—the tilt of the head upward at whoever she

9

was speaking to, partly because she was always shorter than the other person, partly because (Amy saw only now) the posture came off as ingratiating: *I look up to you.* She remembered with unwelcome clarity the tenderness she'd felt toward Dina in the hospital; she wanted to tuck that tilted head, like a child's, to her own body in a gesture of reciprocal support. She had done so more than once. Now the idea repulsed her, though of course she did not show it.

Amy declined the lunch invitation, saying she had too much work to do, and Dina retreated, looking abashed and vexed with herself for having asked. Of course Amy couldn't have told her the truth, which was that even if she *wanted* to have lunch with Dina, she made it a point not to leave the bank premises or walk around town during the workday, when she might run into her former therapist. (Which didn't mean she didn't hope to glimpse the therapist through the bank window someday, when the other woman was unaware of being watched. But it hadn't happened yet.)

On Monday of her third week, Dina came in early, and Amy watched as she pinned up a few maples leaves that had begun turning color, along with some photographs, next to her desk. She swallowed the impulse to tell Dina it was discouraged for bank employees to show personal items where customers could see them. She waited for Dina to put up images of chaos and disorders like kwashiorkor. Surely when she did so, Trevor and the others would see how peculiar she was, and it wouldn't be long before there was a mutual decision that her departure would be for the best.

But no: moving closer, she saw that the photos were of landscapes and seascapes—beautiful pictures, intended to soothe and inspire. Looking around to make sure no one else had come in yet, Amy leaned across the desk and whispered, "These?" as she pointed at a peninsula in blue water, reflecting the brightest of skies.

Dina smiled. "I know. It's a change, for me. But we thought we'd try it." Amy recognized that *we*: it was the way a patient referred to her therapist, the same way a wife might refer to a husband—*we* are one and the same, a united front, do not even think about untangling the separate parts. Amy didn't have a therapist anymore, and now Jack was the other half of her *we*, but she remembered how necessary a comfort that first *we* had been. Dina went on, "I read somewhere that people, potential customers, tend to be motivated by scenes like this. They've done studies. I thought I'd give it a try."

"Well, good luck with it." Amy felt, again, the fraudulent smile on her own face. She sensed Dina watching her as she returned to her desk, though when she looked, the new account representative appeared intent on tacking a waterfall to the wall.

Later that day, Dina and Trevor came back from the sandwich shop giggling together. They stopped when they saw Amy. "What?" Amy asked, trying to give the impression, lighthearted, that she wanted in on the joke.

"Oh, nothing," Trevor said. "You had to be there." He touched Dina's arm and said, "Later, girlfriend," and they laughed again.

Amy went back to her desk feeling her legs numbing beneath her, insisting to herself that she stop perceiving a threat where there was none. She knew Dina; Dina would never tell anyone about the past they had shared. She would not. She would not.

And yet: look at all the other things that had changed since then. Dina had gotten a degree, an apartment, a job only a level or two below Amy's. The pictures she looked at now were pretty ones. Didn't it make sense that other things might have changed, too?

But if she were being honest with herself (though she'd never understood why this was considered such a virtue, it could be so painful), she knew it wasn't the prospect of other people identifying who she'd been once that made her sight go white. The real threat was harder to acknowledge, more shameful to name. The real threat was that she'd become that person again. Worse, that she'd never really been anyone else.

She held her breath and let it out again only when she began to feel light-headed. She hadn't done that in years— her trick for making herself float for a moment above what she wanted to ignore. Self-intoxication, her therapist had called it. *It's bad for you, destructive.*

So? Amy had wanted to say, but she didn't. Only now, holding her breath again, did she remember how good it felt.

She had also forgotten about Dr. Cardoza, until he walked into the bank on the first Wednesday of October, Dina's second month at the bank. *Forgotten* was not really the right word, Amy knew. In the language of psychiatry, you didn't forget, you repressed.

When he'd come in a year earlier to transfer his checking, credit, and retirement accounts from another bank, and to open a college fund for the kids Amy (of course) never knew he had, she hadn't realized who it was in time to hide herself as he sat down at the desk that was now Dina's, with the account representative who'd held the job before her. The doctor had caught Amy peering out from her office, and she blushed, gave a small exclamation she hoped he wouldn't hear, and immediately bent down to pretend she needed something in her bottom drawer. A few minutes later, looking away as she walked past him on her way to the employees' break room, but trying also to gauge his face for recognition, it seemed to her that he sensed she was familiar but couldn't place where he knew her from.

But Dina was another story. She'd been confined to that unit twice before the time she overlapped with Amy, and during one of those times Dr. Cardoza had been her primary. Amy watched as, reaching to shake each other's hands when he approached Dina's desk, they both jerked a little at the contact, understanding only at that moment who the other was. Dina murmured something; the doctor murmured back. Amy waited for him to get up, smile with embarrassed apology, and step away as he looked around for someone else to help him; she waited for Dina to look at him blankly, lip quivering as Amy had seen it do so often in the hospital, always before Dina tried to shut herself in the bathroom but was restrained from doing so. She tried to deny in herself the pleasure she felt in this anticipation—the anticipation of Dr. Cardoza reminding Dina of her place, even in this establishment where he was the customer and she possessed the authority to give or withhold from him the services he desired.

But the doctor did not rise from his seat at Dina's desk. As Amy watched, both of them laughed a bit, and Cardoza gave a little wave as if to say, *That was another time, another world. Water under the bridge.* He leaned across to look at the papers Dina showed him. Asked her some questions. Signed where she indicated, took the copies she peeled off for him. Shook her hand again as he got up, and said (Amy made it a point to listen), "I'm happy to see you looking so well. You've worked hard; you deserve all the good things that are happening to you."

He'd barely exited the building before Dina—who until then had been so careful to avoid letting on to anyone that she knew Amy as someone other than the person who'd hired her—seemed unable to resist jumping out of her seat, scurrying to the edge of Amy's office, poking her head in, and with her crooked grin whispering, "Remember?"

Of course Amy did. She knew Dina was referring to the day Cardoza had filled in for the regular doctor on the women's unit where they were inmates (no, she corrected herself, *inpatients*), and it was his job to lead the morning check-in circle. He wanted everyone to state a personal resolution for that day, and when somebody asked him, *Why don't you start, what's yours?* he shifted in his seat, took a sip of the fancy coffee he'd bought for himself at a shop none of them had access to, and said, "I don't have to give one, I'm not part of the group." His answer had not gone over well, which he no doubt realized even before the first person checking in said that her resolution was to have a better bowel movement than the one she'd had the day before. It was this moment, Amy knew, that Dina referred to as she stood in the doorway after seeing Cardoza out.

Passing Amy's office, he'd looked at her with a flicker of recognition but she believed she was safe, believed he had not identified her as a resident in his psychiatric unit, from all those years ago. She'd lifted her head as he passed her desk, and nodded the way she'd learned to when she met Jack and entered her new life—the life of competent and confident adults, to all appearances equals.

But then she thought she saw the dawning of recognition in Cardoza's face. Was it the context—seeing Dina and Amy together—that caused him to remember he knew both women from the same place? She thought he almost made a noise, an exclamation in realizing, but then checked himself and gave her an awkward, uneasy smile as he passed by.

Dammit, Dina! The words were so loud in her mind that she worried for a moment she'd said them aloud.

A few minutes later Dina and Trevor stopped to ask if she wanted anything when they went to the sub shop. She gave them a curt *No, thank you* and did her best to ignore the look they exchanged when they heard the distress in her voice.

Distress. It was a word her therapist had used often,

because Amy told her how anxious the word *anxiety* made her, and how much she hated the word *depression*. People said they were depressed when it got cloudy, when a dress they wanted didn't come in the right size. They had no idea.

In the cemetery she'd recently taken to driving through on her way home, a couple of teenage boys were already hanging ghosts, made of sheets, in the trees. She watched them until they noticed and began to stare back at her, at which point she plunged into the car and sped out, leaving a skid. At dinner, Jack asked if something was bothering her. It wasn't the first time he'd done so since Dina was hired, but it was the first time Amy sensed that he didn't believe her when she put on her most normal smile and said she was fine, just a little tired. He said he would give Laurel her bath and Amy thanked him and accepted, which she saw surprised him because he'd made this offer often before now but she had always declined.

"Go read your book," he encouraged her, and Amy picked it up from the bedside table and tried. She'd been enjoying the stories, especially the one about the Russian housewife whose talking sugar bowl served as her confessor and therapist, but tonight they seemed too complicated, there was too much on Amy's own mind, so she closed the book and reached for her laptop instead. While the water was running, she searched for anything that popped into her head—what movies were showing, the ten-day forecast, which stores would be having the best Columbus Day sales. The information that presented itself as a result of these searches she did not even register. Then she let her fingers rest on the keys for a long moment before typing the name of her former therapist. She had not allowed herself to do anything like this since her marriage to Jack. (Well, with one exception. A day five years ago when Laurel, then ten months old, had an ear infection and Amy was home with her all day. The antibiotics wouldn't kick in, and nothing Amy could do would soothe the baby, so after six hours straight of listening to the red screams, Amy closed the door to the nursery, took her cell phone outside, blocked her own number from showing on the other end, and dialed the therapist's number, which still came to her by heart. She'd expected only to hear the familiar voice on the machine, but for some reason the therapist answered; later, Amy would wonder whether she'd been aware that she made the call at five minutes before the hour, subconsciously—consciously?—hoping she would get the live and still-cherished person on the other end. "Hello? Yes? Is anyone there?" the therapist demanded, but of course Amy couldn't say anything, and the action of hanging up caused her heart to clutch in the same grief as when she'd had to leave that office at the end of each fifty-minute hour.)

On the computer now, up came the titles of papers the therapist had coauthored since Amy had been her patient, images of her speaking at lecterns, a site for physician ratings that gave her five stars. Amy refrained from looking at any of the photos, knowing it would only add to the distress she already felt. She was about to close the search window, determined to shake herself free of whatever held her and to relieve Jack from bath duty, when at the bottom of the list of items containing the therapist's name she saw the town's police log, and clicked before she could consider whether it was a good idea.

The item was dated a few months earlier, July. A shoplifting incident had been reported at The Blue Flamingo, a boutique around the corner from the therapist's office (Amy had browsed there numerous times, never buying, when she was early for her appointment and did not want to enter the waiting room because she might see the previous patient coming out), and a summons had been issued for the therapist, citing the crime of larceny of property worth more than two hundred fifty dollars.

No, not possible. Not possible either to undo knowing, or to undo the clicks that had led to knowing, and all of it Dina's fault. Amy shut the computer and barged into the bathroom, interrupting a conversation between her husband and daughter. They both looked at her with puzzlement and suspicion, and she laughed to persuade them and herself that she was just in a silly mood. She told Jack she wanted to do the bedtime story, and when Laurel asked her to read it twice and then three times, Amy was only too happy for the distraction. Instead of joining Jack in front of the TV when she was finished, she went back to the bedroom, opened her laptop again, and brought up the bank's database.

She already knew Dina's login number, because Dina kept it on a yellow sticky at the side of her terminal. Same as at the hospital, where there had been yellow stickies everywhere in the room they shared, reminding her to brush her teeth, brush her hair, call her aunt. Trevor had recommended she hide this one (Amy had overheard him), but Dina waved away the suggestion as if to say she didn't need to, she trusted everyone in the branch, and Amy saw that Trevor didn't have the heart to advise her otherwise.

The only thing left to fill in was the password, and this she knew, too, though she hadn't realized it until the moment—now—that it became the thing she sought. On the sticky note underneath the login was the letter *K* followed by a line, as in the old Russian novels she'd read in college that named provinces only by their initials. Amy typed it wrong once, but as soon as she looked up the word and entered the correct spelling—*Kwashiorkor*—up it came, a listing of all the accounts Dina had opened since she joined the bank. She went to Hector Cardoza's first and made some adjustments that were detrimental, but small enough that they would not be discovered right away. She did the same to a dozen other accounts selected at random. Upgraded some to levels that would incur fees those customers were not expecting; eliminated overdraft protection on others; erased existing client orders on a few more. By the time she'd closed the computer again, she felt calm enough to watch the news with her husband, and normal enough to turn toward him instead of away when he reached for her later under the sheets.

That night she didn't think she slept, expecting the door to be pushed open every half hour and a flashlight shined down the length of her body. But she must have slept, because even in the dream she *knew* it was a dream when she found herself arguing with her former therapist in The Blue Flamingo, over a dress displayed in the window: Which of the two of them would it fit best? The therapist suggested that they both try it on and see. Amy felt the familiar, life-saving relief at knowing that one of them had things figured out. But as she reached for the dress and asked if she could take it to the changing room first, the therapist began to laugh. "You don't deserve it, and I'm going to steal it anyway!" she shrieked, showing teeth far bigger and out of proportion with her mouth than in real life—in the dream, the teeth took over her whole face.

A few hours later, in the bank, Dina knocked timidly on Amy's door. The sound made Amy put a hand to her heart; she'd been jumpy all morning, beginning when Laurel banged a cupboard shut. "Don't do that," she'd said, and Laurel and Jack gave her the same look she'd seen on their faces the night before. To avoid encountering it again, she sequestered herself in the bedroom until they both left for the day.

Amy made a weak motion inviting Dina in. "I was thinking about yesterday," Dina said, "when Trevor and I came back from lunch. I was worried you thought we were talking about you, because that's what *I* would have thought. So I just wanted to tell you, that wasn't it. I would never tell anybody how we knew each other—before. I hope you already know that, but just in case, I wanted to say so for sure." Her face flushed from the exertion of generating so many sentences together without a break.

Amy thanked her, hoping she gave off the impression that she didn't quite remember the moment Dina was talking about. Then she added, "I didn't think anything of it. I'm used to not always being included on inside jokes—it comes with the territory of being the boss."

Dina flushed deeper. "Oh, of course. Of course you didn't. Well, forgive me—I'm sorry I brought it up." She bowed her head and backed away, like a subject leaving the presence of royalty.

Amy swiveled in her seat and, holding her breath, logged a second time into Dina's accounts. But presented with all those names and figures, she could not remember the actions she'd performed on them the day before—the little tweaks here and there, the "mistakes" she'd engineered that would appear not criminal, but patently incompetent. She'd kept no record, and there was no way for her to restore the accounts to their original statuses without calling attention to what had been changed. From behind her desk, she looked out at the people who reported to her and at the wide, bright, efficient space that had become a symbol to her of her own fitness and mastery, the esteem she'd swindled from the world. *Act as if you're the person you want to be.* She looked out, but she did not see any of what she knew to be there.

It was Hector Cardoza who triggered the discovery, storming into the bank with his eyes and voice irate as he headed toward Dina's desk. She flinched, leaning back from the force of his accusations, and in the branch manager's absence, Amy had to rush over to reassure him that everything would be fixed. Would he have shown so much anger if the person responsible hadn't been someone he'd treated because she couldn't function the way she was supposed to? Shouldn't this have been a reason for him to hold back? If Amy had anticipated such a reaction from the doctor, she might have held herself back from fiddling with the accounts. Oh, who was she kidding? She would have done what she did anyway.

Dina remained surprisingly stoic—her face impassive, her spine erect—as she withstood Dr. Cardoza's venom, and for the rest of the afternoon, Amy felt both disappointment and relief at the idea that her actions had not borne the results she'd thought they would. But the next morning the branch manager called Dina into his office for a reason only Amy guessed, and she emerged twenty minutes later holding a hand to her head, looking so much as if she might collapse that Trevor went over to help her back to her seat. In keeping with the manager's memo encouraging everyone to wear some kind of costume, Dina had gotten herself up as a bumble bee, and Amy watched her black-and-yellow-striped face shake back and forth, the antennae attached to her head bopping comically as Trevor asked, *What's wrong? What happened?* kneeling beside her in his Tin Man suit.

The manager, who had ignored his own instructions to dress in disguise, left by the back door. Amy knew he would stand outside smoking until Dina was gone. She kept planning to get up and go over to Dina, but her feet would not allow her to stand. After five minutes of sitting at her desk without moving and another five cleaning it out, Dina approached Amy's office, Trevor still hovering, and finally Amy rose to meet them at her door.

"Oh. You're a doctor," Dina said, seeing the stethoscope around Amy's neck. It was Amy's only concession to the costume directive. Smiling bleakly, Dina added, "Just not the kind *we* know."

Amy raised her eyebrows as alarm lit her lungs in a quick singe. Had Dina figured out what she'd done? Was she going to punish Amy now, by revealing everything in front of Trevor, which meant it would be futile to continue trying to hide?

But no: in the next moment she remembered that Dina was a better person than that, she really had only meant it as a private joke, forgetting that Trevor would not understand. Maybe even oblivious to the fact that Trevor stood beside her; maybe even not knowing who he was. When Amy looked closer, she saw in Dina's eyes the quality of confusion and psychic disarray she remembered from the hospital, which had been so impressively absent in the month or more since Dina had held this job, and apparently for some years before. "I'm sorry," Dina said, her bee-face crumpling as she sought out Amy's shoulder. Not knowing how to resist, Amy patted her back as if she were comforting Laurel. Appearing perplexed at Dina's choice of confidante, Trevor retreated. "I should never have thought I could do it," Dina said, the words barely decipherable as her mouth moved against Amy's blouse. Amy thought she was crying, but when Dina pulled her face away to make herself understood better, she noted with relief that this was not the case. "What was I thinking? I can't believe the mistakes he showed me. What made me think I could actually hold down this kind of job?"

Amy shut the door and led her to the seat she'd occupied during their interview a month and a half earlier, but Dina declined to sit. "Does this ever happen to you?" she asked Amy. "You're going along thinking things are okay, maybe *good* even, and then something happens to remind you you're still a—someone who doesn't belong in the real world?"

Amy didn't answer. The response that might have made Dina feel better was the truthful one, but she could not give it. "I'm the one who's sorry," she said. "I mean, that you're feeling this way. Listen, I'll be happy to give you a reference somewhere else." But her failure to join Dina in what she was suffering, she could tell, only made things worse.

At the end of the day, Trevor stopped by her door to say, "Did he have to do it on damn Halloween?" Amy shrugged, an effort to conceal that her shoulders were shaking. "There's just something about her, you know? That makes you want to protect her." He'd discarded the Tin Man costume, but there were still streaks of silver on his face. "Maybe *protect* is the wrong word. But you know what I mean." Amy told him yes, she did, and handed him a tissue so he could remove what remained of his mask.

She stayed in the bank until everyone else had left. On her way out, she saw that Dina had taken with her only the personal items from her desk drawers; the photographs she'd brought in, to inspire herself and her customers, were still tacked to the wall. Casually, as if it didn't mean anything, Amy went over and removed the one that had always caught her eye first, a bank of grass blades inclining toward the sun. Though her impulse was to tuck the paper into her purse, she crumpled it and dropped it into the trash.

At home, Jack was helping Laurel into her costume. He'd already placed a bowl of candy on the table in the foyer. "I'll take her," he told Amy over her protest, avoiding her eyes as their ballerina stepped into her tutu. "You be the hander-outer. Or turn the light off and rest a little. Why don't you take a bath?"

Still looking down, he put Laurel's jacket on over her leotard and zipped it up to her chin. They both told Amy to have fun, then slipped away together before she could beg them not to. The house expanded in its emptiness and went dark. By the time the first steps approached, she'd forgotten they would be coming, and she ignored the knock.

ORIGINAL WORK

The assignment was a five-to-seven-page essay on the question, "Is it worse to be cruel to a dog than to a flea?" When the professor put it up on the whiteboard for the students to copy, a few of them snickered, as if they believed the actual assignment had yet to be written. But when one of the snickerers—a young woman whose right wrist was encircled by the tattoo of a green vine—said, "Really?" the professor turned the inflection around and responded, "Really," before she had even laid her dry-erase pen in the whiteboard bed. She was a woman in her late forties who dressed formally for every class, usually in some skirt and blouse combination, with the same pair of low black pumps. Though her countenance said that she took this all quite seriously—the class, her students, life—there was also about her an air that suggested how quick she might be to relax, even have fun, in a setting other than this austere, purely functional room.

She bid them all a good weekend, which was the signal that they had been granted permission to pack up and leave. The students stood and shuffled in a slow herd toward the door, slow because most of them were running thumbs across the screens in their hands to see what crucial developments might have appeared there in the last hour. The final student in line was a young man who'd sat next to the green-vine tattoo. He approached the professor and cleared his throat, though she had already turned her face to receive whatever it was he would say.

"I don't think I can write five pages on that," he said, nodding at the sentence on the board. "I'm not trying to be rude or anything. Or, like, difficult. But—I mean— five pages?"

"Well, you don't have to write five pages." She moved to the board to erase the assignment without turning her back on him. "You could write seven." She smiled, appearing to take pleasure in her own joke, but let it ebb when he gave out a guffaw that sounded more tortured than amused.

"Look, Stephen," the professor said in a voice that was firm but not unkind, "I won't ask you why you signed up for a philosophy class if you weren't interested in thinking about questions like this. Maybe it's just something you need for your major. But since you're here, you might as well see if you can get something out of it."

"Okay. But I'm pretty sure I won't get five pages." He smiled, having apparently calculated that this particular professor might appreciate his own weak attempt at wit. She urged him again to have a good weekend, and pretended she needed more time to collect her things so that he could leave the room alone ahead of her. He seemed to understand that she was pretending, and why, though it was also clear that he had no way of showing his gratitude.

She had advised them early in the semester that they would all come to find their own ways of thinking about the questions she raised in class. Some of you will be able to concentrate in front of the computer, she said, but for others, a long walk by yourself might be the best bet—your mind will be working on the problems even if you're looking in store windows or up at the sky.

And I'm not talking about a long walk with your cell phone, she added. If you really want to get some good thinking done, leave it behind.

Stephen took his phone out of his pocket and set it on his desk in the room he shared with the boyfriend of the girl adorned with the green vine. Usually when he came out of the dormitory, he turned right, in the direction of the classroom buildings and the cafeteria, but now he went the opposite way and walked toward the little town that bordered the campus. He had only been to the town once, the day his parents dropped him off at college two months before. They'd gone for lunch at a diner called The Brown Cow, after which his parents would get back into the freshly emptied car and make the five-hour return drive home. During lunch, his mother kept up her hypercheerfulness to the extent that neither Stephen nor his father could get a word in edgewise, but when the waitress came to clear the plates away, his father lost it. They stayed at the table longer than they should have, so he could collect himself. But every time it seemed he had done so, the crying started again, and he reached for another napkin from the dispenser. When she saw what was going on, the waitress, who was his mother's age, told them there was no hurry, and she patted both Stephen and his father on the shoulder.

Stephen crossed the street before he would have had to pass The Brown Cow, and kept his eyes trained on the sidewalk. His face held the look of someone straining to identify a tune he could hear only faintly. He walked more than a mile, beyond the point at which the street with the shops ended, then turned and retraced his steps back to campus, still appearing to listen for the tune.

He sat down at his desk, consulted the notebook in which he had copied the assignment, and created a new document on his computer. He watched the cursor blink for a few minutes, then leaned back in his chair. After a few more minutes he leaned forward and typed, "It is worse to be cruel to a dog than to a flea. This is because a dog will understand that a person is being cruel to him, and a flea will not." He read it over and considered before inserting "probably" before "a flea will not." Then he tabbed to a new paragraph and wrote, "That's all I got," laughed to himself in a way that did not sound remotely happy, erased the line, and put the computer to sleep.

In the cafeteria, his roommate and the roommate's girl-friend called Stephen over to join them. "That assignment is bogus," Amber said. When she waved her fork at Stephen to emphasize how much she meant what she was saying, a dot of ketchup landed on her wrist, looking like a ladybug crawling through the green vine. "Who cares about fleas? Do you? I wouldn't mind being cruel to a flea. You're *supposed* to be cruel to fleas, right? Do they serve any purpose other than being a pain in the ass?"

"I don't know." Stephen's expression indicated that he would have liked very much to offer a more intriguing response.

"I think it's a trick question." Amber spoke around a mouthful of French fries, and Stephen looked away.

"I don't think so. She isn't like that."

"Well, I'm going to treat it as if it's a trick. Here's my essay answer right here: 'Yes. It is worse to be cruel to a dog than to a flea.' That's the whole thing." She started to choke on her own laughter and her boyfriend clapped her on the back. "Don't you dare steal it!" she warned Stephen, when she had recovered. "Don't you plagiarize me."

Stephen told her he wouldn't. "That's not really what I'm going to do, doofus," she said, winding her finger through the remaining ketchup on her plate and licking it off. "What do you take me for? What I'm really going to do is type in a search for 'cruelty + philosophy,' and whatever comes up, I'll change a few words and voilà! Instant paper."

"Yeah, just do that," his roommate told Stephen. "Why not?"

Seeming eager to offer evidence of her strategy's success, Amber went on, "That's how I finished that World Lit assignment, some crazy Russian book about a woman who has conversations with her sugar bowl. I mean, *excuse* me?

But it turns out there's a ton of critical stuff on it! All mine for a click. Who knew?"

Stephen shrugged—but it was not the shrug of someone who didn't care. He stood and picked up his tray. His roommate asked, "Hey, you meeting up with us later at the Brat? That girl from Western Civ told Amber she'd be there."

Amber told Stephen, "She doesn't know who you are yet. But she will." She pointed at him as if making him a promise.

"Maybe," he said.

"Don't be a pussy." His roommate pointed at him, too. "It's Friday night. You're supposed to go out and get wasted, not sit in some crap dorm room and do crap work. That's bullshit." He sat back, seeming surprised by his own vehemence.

"Thanks," Stephen told them, turning.

"For what?" Amber said, but he was far enough away by then that he didn't need to answer.

By Sunday afternoon he had scribbled many notes to himself, but no actual pages. When his roommate went to meet Amber for dinner, Stephen got up from his desk and looked out the window. It was a gray day, dismal with a light sleet, and the outside lights had been on since morning at The Brown Cow and other places on the main street. He went back to his computer and typed in "cruelty + philosophy," but closed the search engine before it could launch.

When his mother called that evening, he told her he'd spent the weekend working on his philosophy paper but was having some trouble. The way he put it was that he didn't know what angle to take on it.

His mother said, "Why don't you write to Miranda? She could probably help."

"I thought you wanted me to think for myself. 'That's the whole point of college,' you said."

"We *do* want that. I'm not saying she should give you the answer. But she's your cousin and she's smart. She studied this stuff. It didn't get her anywhere—she's working at a TJ Maxx, for God's sake—but she'd probably jump at the chance to dig back into it again." On the other end of the line he could hear her rummaging through a drawer. "Aunt Cherry just gave me her email address. Here it is, I'll send it to you. By the way, Dad wants to say hi."

A fumbling as the phone changed hands. "You there, Son? What's the problem?"

"There's no problem."

"It sounded as if you needed help with something."

"No. Just writing a paper. Philosophy. It's hard, but that's what college is supposed to be, right?"

His father gave a little snort. "Well, *I* wouldn't know."

"It's okay. I got it covered."

"You sure? Because you know we want to do whatever we can, right?" Then came the choke in his voice that signaled the start of what had waylaid them all at The Brown Cow that day. "Very proud of you, Son," he said, but he had to hand the phone back before he could get it all out.

Two days later he came back from Western Civ and found an email from his cousin with an attachment labeled *Stephen paper*. He clicked on it, read, then took a breath and went to the window. The sky had brightened since the weekend, and the air was lighter, not so dense. He opened the window slightly as his roommate came in. "Come to the Brat, asshole, it's Nickel Beer Night," he said to Stephen. "Aren't you done with that crap paper *yet*?"

"Almost." His roommate waited, just standing there. After a moment, Stephen said, "Okay" and turned the computer off, its shutting-down sound almost covering the sound of his exhalation as before him the screen went dead.

*　　*　　*

The professor had told them she'd return their papers at the end of class a week later. The topic that day was free will versus determinism. An energetic debate rose up between the majority of class members, who voted for free will, and two or three others who argued that every human action is controlled by a causal chain of events leading up to it.

"Stephen, you haven't weighed in yet," the professor said, during a rare pause in the exchange of emphatic comments that all seemed aimed at winning something or beating someone, rather than exploring the different perspectives of an idea.

A flush lit Stephen's neck. "Sorry," he muttered, appearing only then to pay attention to the discussion. "I'm not sure which I believe."

"Nothing wrong with that." The professor gave him an approving look. "Philosophy is a love of seeking wisdom, not a love of having concluded and shut off one's mind. Nice job, everyone." She moved to her desk. "I wish I could say the same for all these papers," she told them all, picking up the stack. "Some *are* very good. But one or two of them made me think I should suggest a new core education course to the administration. Something along the lines of 'How to Hide What You've Googled So It Sounds Like Original Work.'" She paused, standing before the girl with the green vine. Amber reached for her paper, her tattoo sticking out of her sleeve, but the professor held on to it as she continued. "I mean really, people. It's as if you think I might not have a computer or something. Do you think I don't deal with this every semester? It's disheartening, to say the least. And destructive to yourself, though I doubt you would understand why." Finally she let Amber have what she wanted, though by then Amber had covered her face with her hair.

"You can expect a follow-up email from the Academic Integrity Board," the professor said. She did not look at

Amber, but it was clear whom she was speaking to.

Stephen received his paper with the circled blue *A* and did not get up from his seat until everyone else had left the room. The professor did not seem surprised that he had hung back. "Perhaps needless to say, I wasn't expecting the quality of your paper," she told him, erasing the *Pro Free Will* section of the whiteboard. "After you told me it would be so difficult. Did it turn out to be, in the end?" She moved over to *Pro Determinism*, managing to clear the words without turning her back on him.

"I worked really hard on it."

"I'm sorry?"

"I worked really hard on it, I said." He cleared his throat. She had finished wiping the board and was placing her things in the leather satchel she always brought to class.

"Forgive me for asking. It's just that I hadn't seen enough of your work yet to know you could write something like that." She smiled. "I'm impressed. I'll have to call on you more often from now on—it's your own fault for showing me what you're capable of." When he made no move to pack up himself, she told him she'd see him on Thursday, gave a little wave with another smile, and left the room.

Stephen folded the paper over three times and stuck it in his back pocket. Outside it had turned colder than when he'd gone into class, but he continued to carry his jacket instead of putting it on. He walked to The Brown Cow, where he sat at the counter and ordered two milkshakes, which he drank very fast. Then he ordered two more. The waitress he recognized from the day his parents had left him said, "Whoa, honey, you'll make yourself sick," but he shook his head without replying as he drained the big glasses. He left her his last twenty-dollar bill on a check for ten, then slipped out of the diner before she could call him back to tell him he'd made a mistake.

On his way back to campus, he ran into Amber and his

roommate. Amber was crying into her boyfriend's coat. "This is so fucking *bogus*." She turned to Stephen with an expression that indicated she was waiting for him to agree. When he didn't, her face flashed with fresh anger. "That bitch is going to be sorry she did that to me. Just wait till my father gives her a call."

Stephen nodded and began walking up the hill. He stopped and threw up into a trash barrel, and when he straightened again, the girl from Western Civ was watching him with a hand over her own mouth and a look of disgust in her eyes. He walked a few steps farther to sit on a bench. It was still wet from the rain overnight, and he swore and stood quickly, walking back to the bin he'd been sick in. He pulled the paper out of his pocket. *It is just as wrong to be cruel to a flea as to a dog because both of them are creatures. As human beings, we have a moral obligation to show humanity to our fellow creatures, even if our potential victim does not recognize cruelty or cannot feel pain.* He dropped it on top of the trash. A later page was now visible to anyone who might walk by and feel inclined to read part of a philosophy paper thrown out in a puddle of puke. *A moral person who violates his own humanity will be damaged by what he has done, regardless of whether anyone else knows about it, and in ways he will likely not have been able to anticipate.*

He went back to his dorm room and slept through the rest of the day. When his mother called that night, he didn't answer. It wasn't until the weekend that he called her back to tell her he was sorry, he'd been busy. When she asked about the paper and he told her he'd gotten an *A*, she said, "Oh! I knew you could do it, honey. Aunt Cherry will be so pleased, and I'm sure Miranda would love to see what you did with her input." Then he had to hold the phone away from his ear as she repeated the news to his father, and across the distance, both of his parents cheered.

PROVIDENCE

I boarded the train with trepidation: Would I find a space next to the window, with no one occupying the aisle seat next to me? They were rare to come by, but I'd arrived at the platform early, near the head of the line. With that advantage, one could slip into the desired seat, stash a suitcase or courier bag on its adjacent twin, then immediately pretend to be asleep. I've noticed that most riders entering a train car are reluctant to ask a sleeping person if the seat next to him or her is free. Of course, some people don't mind "waking" one up at all. "Is somebody sitting here?" they demand to know, all the more loudly because the one in the seat might, while feigning sleep, also be listening to music through a pair of headphones.

I had no such accessory, however. Though of course an unaccompanied woman must exercise caution in deciding whether to close her eyes for any length of time in a public space, I chose to stick to the simple "sleep" charade, and found to my relief and pleasure that no one sat with me through the first two stops out of Boston's South Station. The train was headed to New York City, and I was tense, partly because Amtrak had only just begun running again after the attacks. But my anxiety had more to do with the people I was about to meet, one of whom was the man who may or may not turn out to be the editor of a manuscript I'd written. That is, the house he worked for had almost, but not quite, decided to publish my book, a collection of the fiction of Anya Chaykovskaya, a contemporary Russian writer whose work was obscure in her own country. She'd been born in Moscow in 1955, ten years to the day before my own birth in Buffalo. She published her first pieces in the waning days of perestroika, and produced one short book—a "slim volume," as it is said—but after that she'd only placed occasional pieces in literary journals. I'd had the good fortune to come across a few of her untranslated stories early in my graduate program in Slavic literature, and after reading the first one—depicting a woman who sits at her kitchen table one day to find her sugar bowl asking provocative questions about the way she is conducting her life—I was hooked.

My book would be the first volume containing all of her work, in addition to my accompanying analytical essays. The publisher liked it, but he insisted that the subject, Chaykovskaya herself, approve the project. They had sent her the manuscript, and indicated to me that her response was positive; before she would proceed with the authorization, however, she had arranged this trip to America, specifically to meet with the editor and me.

The book could make or break my career, my old dissertation advisor had informed me, depending on the critical response. It was so rare as to be unheard of, the discovery of creditable Russian texts that hadn't already been translated into English by Riva Druskin. How had Chaykovskaya's missed her? Somehow, she'd slipped through the cracks.

Whatever the reason, it was not my problem; it was my lucky break. Though I knew better, it was difficult for me not to look ahead and imagine a time when I might not have to subsist on three separate adjunct teaching jobs, tenure-track openings in Slavic studies being hard to come by. As I had been a linguistics minor, the definition of *adjunct* was never far from my mind: *that which is added to something else as a supplement, rather than an essential part.*

I'd had no luck so far with the few applications I'd put

in, but an acclaimed book introducing a previously unrecognized Muscovite author—and a female one, to boot—would no doubt make me a shoo-in for the next available post. Along with the elevation in faculty rank would come more money and (though I knew there was no real correlation here, I believed it anyway) someone to love, honor, and grow old with; in short, a real life. The significance of the dinner waiting at the end of this train trip lodged an anxious weight in my chest as the car clattered over the rails. Would I stammer or have an anxiety attack? Had Chaykovskaya appreciated the whole of my manuscript, or would she find fault with some of my translations, my interpretations, my conjecture about where she would come to stand in Russian letters? Her stature should be high, I argued in the text, especially given her relative youth and the promise of works yet to come. I could see no reason for our meeting to be anything other than cordial; still, one frets.

I sat with my head against the backrest, eyes closed, trying to appear unapproachable.

This seemed to work for the forty-five minutes it took us to reach the next stop, which was Providence. Unfortunately, at that station, my luck ran out.

"Excuse me," the woman said, hovering over me like a bad and dangerous dream. "May I sit with you?" She was tall, like me, and also had blond hair—not unattractive, though she had not picked the best pair of eyeglasses for the shape of her face. I once had someone explain to me the best types of eyeglasses to buy for the shape of one's face, so I knew. This woman had a square face, but the glasses were oval. (I myself wear contact lenses, except on those days when they don't fit right and my vision is blurred.)

"Of course," I responded, smiling as if I had just been waiting for someone to join me. As protective of my space and solitude as I am, I do not like to be rude. "I'm Aisling," I added, as the woman settled into the aisle seat with her purse in her lap.

"Oh, I know," she said, nodding, removing a peppermint candy from the purse and unwrapping it to place in her mouth.

"What do you mean, you *know*?" There was no way she could have guessed my name. Most people I meet can't even pronounce it the correct way, *Ashling*, unless I happen to be in Ireland, where my parents claim I was conceived by accident on their honeymoon.

When the blond woman didn't answer after a moment, I said to her, "What's *your* name?" and she looked around us to make sure no one was listening before she whispered, "I am your addiction." Then she started humming a tune that felt familiar, though I had never heard it before.

"What do you mean, you're my *addiction*?" I didn't bother to keep my voice down, because clearly she was the crazy one. But several people in the car turned and said "Ssh" or put a finger over their mouths.

"I knew you wouldn't believe it," the woman said. "If you want, you can call me Aisling, too." (I heard it as *Aisling II*, before understanding it in the way she meant.) "It's such a pretty name, and you've probably never met another one in your life."

"But that can't really be *your* name, too."

She shrugged. "It's as close as any, for our purposes. Today." She pointed with her eyes at my courier bag. "Is that your book?"

"How do you know about my book?"

She shrugged again. "I know everything about you. Haven't you ever heard that saying at the meetings you go to—the one about how, while you're trying to stay sober, your addiction is perched on your shoulder doing push-ups

35

to stay strong? Just waiting for the day you decide to sabotage yourself, and it can take you under?"

"Okay, so I have heard that," I said. I hadn't been to a meeting in weeks, but it was a popular image among the other recovering alcoholics in my group.

"Well, it's true. Except sometimes we take a break from the push-ups and appear in your life to warn you away from us. Not all of us will do this—some of us are complete assholes, every minute of every day. But I'm one of the nicer ones. And I'm trying to help you." She tried to wipe a look of sanctimoniousness from her mostly featureless face, but didn't quite succeed before I noticed.

"If I ever needed a drink," I commented, not feeling up to completing the sentence: *it would be now.*

"Remember the summer you were fourteen, and you snuck a glass of wine from your parents' party, and you caught a buzz and thought, *This is it—this is the secret to life?*" asked Aisling Jr., as I had come to think of her.

"Yes, I remember that."

"And the times in college you *don't* remember, and the times you got sick in people's cars, and the times you promised yourself and your family, your mentors and your friends, that you would stop?" Aisling Jr. was sucking her peppermint so mightily, I was afraid she might inhale it and choke. Then what position would *I* be in—that of being forced to save my own addiction, instead of letting it die?

"I remember." I reached down to touch my courier bag for the solidity it offered, in this most unusual and discomfiting of circumstances. "Excuse me, but what is the point?" I asked, rubbing the suede between my fingers, thinking of Anya Chaykovskaya and wondering what she would make of all this.

Because, in fact, her stories tended toward the fabulous and the surreal—such as the one about the housewife undergoing a moral interrogation by her sugar bowl. As someone who prefers to read fiction about things that could actually happen in the world I inhabit myself, I almost didn't open Chaykovskaya's book when I came across it in the library and read the description on the dust cover. And indeed I did find her premise to be, at first, disappointingly simplistic: the housewife was merely an ordinary woman in need of counsel in her life.

But plowing deeper into her text, seeking the most accurate English words to stand in for the Russian phrases, I saw how sophisticated the work actually was. For years the housewife had been doing her best to reject understanding that her life was unappealing (no, it was tragic!), though—as these things go—she had not succeeded. The sugar bowl represented the woman's greatest temptation: to acknowledge reality even though this would come at a great cost, because she did not feel she was in a position to change it. Every time she tried to get up from the table to remove herself from its seductive scent, a question came from the bowl that made it impossible for her to ignore (e.g., "Do you really believe the things you tell yourself when you wake up in the middle of the night? Or do you understand that they are illusions, without which you cannot return to sleep?"). In the story, it was not clear whether the sugar bowl actually possessed magical powers or its speech was a projection of the housewife's psyche. Regardless, their conversation was not unlike the one I was having with Aisling Jr. right now, and I wondered if somehow my obsession with Chaykovskaya and her stories was responsible for conjuring the person (apparition?) who sat next to me, crunching away on her sweet.

"The point is that you summoned me here," the false Aisling told me.

"I? Summoned you?"

Beside me she gave a great sigh, as if weary of my question when it had only just been uttered. It occurred to me to wonder if I shared her with other people—in which case she was likely accustomed to, and bored by, the need to explain herself—but the idea that my addiction would not, in fact, be unique to me was not one I wished to continue entertaining. So I decided that I must just be a hard case to convince.

"Yes, you summoned me," she repeated. "Last night, when you were wondering if this book would be published, and you thought of that glass of wine, remember? How good it would feel going down, and how much you needed relief from your apprehension? From the bad visions of what your life will become if they turn you down? I knew it was time for me to visit."

"I did want it," I murmured. "The relief you mention."

"And tonight, what will you do when this editor and your Russian friend sit down and order drinks with their dinners?" My companion pushed the egg-shaped eyeglasses up to sit more securely on her delicate nose. "Won't you want one, too?"

"Of course I will. But I'll order tonic. It's what I always do." I had been sober for four years, since my thirty-first birthday. There had been many dinners, many anxieties, during that time. If this woman really did have access to everything about me, wouldn't she know that?

Without responding to my question, Aisling Jr. put her own head back, looking straight ahead at the seat in front of her. I felt pleased with myself, as if I had said something to give her considerable pause. And if she really *were* my addiction, what a high, to confound the very thing that had caused me such turmoil in my earlier life!

But she didn't stay silent for long. "You denied me," she said, so quietly that I almost didn't hear it.

"What?"

"You denied me. Last night. When you were thinking about this evening, and how nice it would be to have a drink, it occurred to you that I might have gone underground, or even disappeared altogether." She turned her head only slightly, but her eyes locked straight onto mine. "And you thought that maybe there is no such thing as an addiction, only weakness, and if so, you are perhaps strong enough to handle it now. Didn't you?"

"You know, I've had about enough of this," I told her, rising from my seat and preparing to step over her insubstantial legs into the aisle of the train. "I'm going to get a snack from the café car, and when I come back, I want you out of here." I kept my voice low, as she had, so that nobody might hear us. Still, a man in the seat across from us looked up with raised eyebrows from *The Providence Journal*, when he heard what he must have perceived to be a threat issued by me.

"You can't get rid of me by wishing," Aisling Jr. whispered back.

"You're not even real! You don't even exist!" I hissed, and this time other faces turned from the front of our car to see what was happening. I wobbled my way in the opposite direction toward the café, where I stood behind a woman who ordered a six-ounce bottle of wine with her turkey sandwich. The sight of the little bottle made my mouth water, and I had the fleeting image of yanking it from the woman's hand, but when it came my turn, I asked only for pretzels and a Sprite. I would show Aisling Jr., I thought.

As it happened, though, I didn't have to worry any further about her or her judgments. Balancing my snack items as I tried to stay upright in the hurtling car, I managed to make it back to my seat, which I didn't recognize at first because the cushion next to it—where the false Aisling had been sitting—was empty. I sat down, not daring to believe that she had heeded my entreaty to leave, thinking she might just be using the restroom. I looked out the window as I consumed my appetizer, and saw the little town of Mystic pass by with its pretty coast. A woman walking her dog near the water waved at the train. This struck me as unexpectedly poignant and quaint, like something out of a nineteenth-century novel, and I waved back, even as I realized that of course it was too late by then for her to see me.

"Your friend got off at Mystic," the man reading the newspaper said. "She seemed a bit crestfallen, if you ask me."

"She was not my friend," I told him, wondering why I bothered. "She was a stalker, is what she was."

"Funny, she didn't look like one." He mumbled as if fearful of my reaction, hiding behind the horoscopes and the cartoons. "If you looked closely, she could have been your twin."

When Aisling Jr. didn't return by the time we passed New Haven, I breathed a sigh of relief, recalling for some reason a distant Russian tune from one of my first lessons in learning the language. The song tells the story of a boy who is afraid of falling from a horse, but he goes on to become a champion rider famous for *never* falling, because the fear—which remains constant—keeps his vigilance keen. I began humming, and checked to see if I was bothering the newspaper reader, but his seat was empty. How had he managed to leave without my noticing? But I had other things on my mind and did not pursue the question.

I arrived at Penn Station feeling as nervous as ever; the encounter with Aisling Jr.—or whatever her name was—had distracted me for a while, but now it was time for me to meet Chaykovskaya and the editor from the publishing house. They had chosen a restaurant near the station for my convenience because, as I had to teach the next day, I was not staying over in the city but turning right around, after dinner, and taking the late train back home. Originally, I'd dreaded the long night this would mean for me, but as I exited the station, I realized how glad I was, in light of how badly (I now understood) I *did* want a drink, not to have the "out" of a hotel room, afterward, to crash in. I would have to keep my wits about me, in order to meet the right train at the assigned track at the appointed hour.

I found the establishment with little trouble, checked the lobby to see if they were there yet (I had met the editor before, and seen photos of Chaykovskaya), and when they weren't, I sat in the lounge to wait. A server offered me the wine list, but I gave him a smile and demurred. No one watching would have been able to tell how difficult this was for me to do—to send him away—but when he had gone to another table, I felt a surge of accomplishment and thought, *This might not be so bad, after all.* It occurred to me to wonder if perhaps Aisling Jr. had something to do with it—if, in fact, she had placed some kind of protective blessing on me before departing the train. Then I remembered that I didn't believe in such things. She had been a figment of my stress and imagination, nothing more. How to explain the fact that the man reading the newspaper had also seen her was not a question I cared to dwell upon, so I lifted my face, still with the smile on it, to look out again at the lobby.

And thus I was smiling when Chaykovskaya spotted me from across the room. Though the heels of her shoes were thin and steep, she swept rather than tottered toward me with arms outstretched, an ebony pashmina draped fashionably over one shoulder of an orange dress; she let me take in this image, this vivid marriage of dark and bright, as she beheld my own rather stiff presentation in brown suit and unstylish (though recently polished) flats. Then she leaned forward to kiss both of my cheeks in the style of Russian intimates. "Aileen," she said, and I did not take pains to correct her; she could call me whatever she wanted, and "Aileen" was close enough.

Her hair slid down her back in an array of black-gray curls, and her eyes had been rimmed in kohl to accentuate the dark pierce of her gaze. From observing her close up, I could tell that the photographs I had seen of her had been doctored to remove wrinkles, crows' feet, worry lines, or whatever you wish to call them. At first this felt disappointing, until it occurred to me that any Russian writer worth his or her salt should, even in this day and age, exhibit signs of at least some psychic attrition, if not outright suffering.

"Here she is," Anya Chaykovskaya said to the editor, a bland-looking and quiet-voiced man named Morton Hill. "The girl who is to make my fame in America, *da*?" My heart vaulted; shouldn't I take this as an indication that she intended the book deal to go through?

"It would seem so," Morton said to us, with a smile I read in my uncertainty as non-committal; but that could have just been his style. "This way, ladies—I've arranged our table."

We sat in an enclosed back booth I assumed Morton had procured by way of a tip to the maître d', to ensure both our privacy and the freedom for Chaykovskaya to smoke the pastel Russian cigarettes she removed from her sequined clutch and set next to her plate. From time to time she tapped the purse as if to make sure it was still there, or as if it were some kind of talisman she needed to touch every so often in order to feel secure. This surprised me, because I had come to think of her as the kind of accomplished and confident woman I wished I could be, myself. To be honest, during the years I'd spent writing about her work, she had become my idol.

It was to my perturbation, then, that I noticed Chaykovskaya couldn't seem to take her eyes off me. "But you are so young, *da*?" she asked me, and I replied in Russian, "Ten years younger than you," and remarked upon the fact that we shared a birthday. "*Da!*" she said again, seeming delighted, then leaned in and, with a wink as she lit up her fourth cigarette in twenty minutes, called me the Russian word for *sister*.

Morton informed me that because Anya's English was not strong, they had used an interpreter to converse in his editorial offices, just before coming to meet me. Because of the language problem, she'd had to depend on a friend and fellow writer in Moscow—who was fluent in English—to report on my translations of her work and the way I had portrayed her life in my manuscript. To my rising excitement she told me, in Russian (using a phrase that means, roughly, "over the moon"), that she was thrilled with what I had done, and that it honored her greatly to be the subject of such a fine book.

Trying not to let on how ecstatic her words made me (wasn't it better to act as if I had presumed, all along, that this was how the evening would proceed?), I told her, in her mother tongue, how pleased I was to hear her response. "I wanted to get the images just right, and maintain the integrity of the stanzas . . . and in the stories, I hoped to depict each emotion as precisely as you intended." I mentioned the housewife-and-sugar-bowl story specifically, and she seemed captivated by my comments. The story was one of her own favorites, she said, although to be honest—here she leaned in and gave me a wink—the talking sugar bowl had been an accident of sorts, the result of too much Stoli one evening before she'd sat down to write. Then came another wink, so that to this day I can't be sure whether she was pulling my leg. She continued in rapid Russian, which I of course could follow, but which Morton could not, so after a while I paused and told him that, yes, everything seemed to indicate a green light for the deal.

The server appeared at our elbows; Morton ordered champagne, and when three flutes were set down, I said nothing, as I usually did, about having mine taken away. My lips were numb and my heart was full, and in that moment I told myself that I deserved to celebrate—didn't I? Wouldn't it have dampened the moment—indeed, mightn't it have affected, adversely, their opinion of me—if I refused to raise a glass to seal our communion? Surely I'd heard enough stories, at the meetings I went to, about binges and their resulting disasters ("jackpots," as the meeting lingo went) that I would heed those warnings, and guard against such things happening to me. When the champagne had been poured, we all toasted Chaykovskaya, then me, then Morton, who said he would send out the contracts tomorrow. The first taste made me close my eyes in what can only be described as elation, and I thought, *Ah*, there *you are; how* much *I've missed you.* I tried to sip discreetly, but the glass was small and easily emptied. Morton ordered a bottle of wine, three more glasses were brought, and we finished it before the food arrived at the table. When the entrées came, so did another bottle, and then a third. I was feeling warm and in love with life, and by the time we had finished eating, it seemed we were all quite drunk. It impressed and daunted me, then made me jealous, that although Chaykovskaya herself put away more than her fair percentage of the pinot, her speech and demeanor skipped not a beat. My own cells had been so long deprived that they responded to the novelty of the intoxicants by kicking up their heels and turning handsprings through my roused blood.

After Irish coffee with the tiramisu, Morton excused himself to make a phone call. Anya and I giggled like schoolgirls; I accepted one of her mint-colored Sobranies, and in the few inches between our bent-together heads as she lit it for me, she confessed that she'd had another reason, besides the disposition of my manuscript, to visit New York. For the past year she'd been flirting via email messages with a novelist who lived in Connecticut, and he had urged her to make the trip so that they could consummate their affair. Which they had done that very afternoon, she confided, lowering her voice and readjusting the shawl that had fallen away from the shoulder of her orange dress. She'd been late leaving the hotel room to meet up with Morton at the publishing house.

After telling me this, she paused, her eyes expectant and downright sly as she waited for me to indicate my desire for her to give further details. I understood that I was already out of my league in the burgeoning friendship, indeed in the language of women, as the closest I'd ever come to a relationship was a series of desultory dates arranged by my best friend in graduate school, with her boyfriend's roommate, which ended when I puked on him in bed one night when he asked me to get on top. I'd gone out with a few men since getting sober, but nothing ever seemed to last. One of them had told me once that I was a difficult person to get to know, that I seemed to have a chip on my shoulder he couldn't name or get beyond (though he said he wanted to), but I chalked it up instead to the fact that people outside academia tend to be intimidated by the people inside it.

My response—or rather, the lack of one—put Anya off, and I wanted to say, *Wait! Please don't turn away—I thought we were friends; even sisters, remember?* I began to realize, as guilt and dread raised their hammers, just how inebriated I was. "Well," she said, clearly understanding now that the best thing to do was to put a period at the end of her story about the affair and try not to regret telling it, "We both realized we'd been fooling ourselves. It was a— how would you say it? A phantasm." Then, charitably, or (I cringed inside to think) out of boredom, she changed the subject. "You know, Aileen," she said, and I sensed it was the last round of energy she'd be able to muster in my direction, "I looked you up before they sent me this book of yours. I found the paper you wrote on Brodsky, the explication you did of *Less Than One*. I found it quite brilliant. Based on that, even before I received your manuscript, I decided that if it was even halfway decent, I would put up my thumb for it." She made the gesture with one hand while with the other she stubbed her butt out, though there was barely room for it in the ashtray by now. Reaching for another cigarette, she found she had run out, clucked in impatience, and began looking around the room to find something as interesting as the nicotine had been.

Panicked that I was losing her—and desperate to restore the rapport she appeared now to wish she hadn't offered—I blurted out, "I stole it," though I'd had no idea that these were the words preparing to emerge. Well, I had her attention now, that was for sure; she stared at me with a frown, as if thinking she couldn't have heard right. Impaired as I was, I still knew full well that I had stepped to the edge of a precipice, but the drive to pull myself back to safety was not as strong as the desire to reciprocate a secret, as if in that way I could win her back. I heard myself continue: "The article on Brodsky. I found it in a journal so obscure, I knew nobody would notice. I changed the wording, of course. I also checked to make sure that the person who wrote it was dead." It would not have been an exaggeration to say that I only barely realized it was me who was speaking. This was a sensation that had once been so familiar that those times I was sober, and in control of what I was saying, had felt foreign to me. "It's one of my talents, finding things in libraries nobody else knows is there. It's how I found your book in the first place. When I opened it the first time, the dust made me sneeze."

Why had I said those things? Too late, I remembered that *confession* is not a synonym for *intimacy*. As I watched Chaykovskaya's face settle slowly into an expression of comprehension, anger, and distaste, I felt my core wither and begin to wilt. I recognized what I had just told her as part of my history, but on the other hand, I had worked so hard during these past four years to repair myself and the damages I had committed up to that point (in the process doing my best to erase the shame they engendered) that in my currently drunken state I could no longer be sure of which was the real me. I tried to explain how insecure and afraid I had been as a graduate student, and how I'd persuaded myself that the author of the Brodsky article, being deceased, couldn't be hurt anymore, but I found my tongue tripping over words that spilled forth in a nonsensical combination of Russian and English.

For a moment in which I felt suspended above myself, Chaykovskaya beheld my confusion. Then, dropping her voice so that I had to lean closer to listen, she asked, "Are you telling me this because it's the truth? Or are you just so drunk you don't know what you're saying?"

She was giving me a chance, I understood. I could take it all back and still get what I wanted—*everything* I wanted— and she would pretend that she believed me, for the sake of our mutual good. Or I could leave what I'd said on the table between us, and my lack of a denial would speak for itself, to the point that neither of us could ignore it.

I tried. I tried desperately to laugh as if I had meant only to make a joke, to assert what a fool I was—a *durak*, in her language—but instead I began to vomit into my napkin. At this, Chaykovskaya stood up, signaling to Morton that he should hurry, she was ready to go.

I let the napkin fall under the table as he paid the bill. Clearly he was aware that something had happened between us two women, but of course he had no idea what it was, and over my efforts to tell him that everything was fine, and that I would look for the publishing agreement by fax the next morning, my heroine took him aside and began speaking in rapid Russian. I could see that he understood the gist though not the words themselves, but I caught them all in their dismaying vehemence: *credentials*, *fraud*, *Druskin*, and (I felt my heart go cold) *cancel*. They walked ahead of me out of the restaurant, and by the time we'd reached the sidewalk, the visages they both turned to me were no longer celebratory, but stern. Morton said he would call me the next day, but I already knew what it was he would have to say. When I tripped on a crack in the sidewalk, he reached out to steady me, looking sad and concerned, but Chaykovskaya clucked again and pulled him farther away from me, until they were figures in the distance and I had to run, stumbling, to meet the last train.

On board, I didn't try my trick of finding two empty seats. After what had happened on the way down, I preferred the company of a real human being, and asked if I could sit next to a teenage boy with buds in his ears. He shrugged and moved over to the window, wrinkling his nose as I plopped down beside him, exhaled hugely, and let my head fall back in despair.

"Shit, shit, shit," I murmured, but perhaps not quietly enough, because the earbud boy heard me and tried to conceal his smile. Not knowing what else to do, I made my way to the bar car and bought two little bottles of wine, which were all they would sell to a single person at one time. I sat at a table and drank the wine out of the plastic cup the barman had given me. I closed my eyes and waited for the alcohol to do its forgetting work.

"Believe me now?" a voice said, and I did not have to open my eyes to know that Aisling Jr. was back. But when I looked around, I didn't see her. "Check your shoulder," she said, and letting my glance fall, I saw her in miniature, doing squat-thrusts on my blazer sleeve.

"Can you tell me how to fix things?" I asked, but I was not surprised when the answer I got back was a shake of the head. "I tried. You had your chance," she said, and the smile accompanying these words was a chilling amalgam of delight and sadness. Then she gave a little laugh and I tried to flick her off, but no force could remove her from my shoulder. When I shrugged out of the blazer, she attached herself to my skin. As I watched, she grew smaller and smaller until she was no bigger than a freckle. But still I could feel her working hard to keep her strength up, for the day she would deliver the knockout blow I no longer had the power to resist.

THE SYDNEY OPERA HOUSE

Insufficient sleep. A virus. An infection. Tiny crystals of calcium floating around in her ear canal. Stress.

These are the possible reasons the doctor gives for why Petra is dizzy.

"What about a brain tumor?" She knows from her Internet search that this is unlikely, but it's the explanation she feels most attached to. If someone asked her why, she'd be embarrassed to tell the truth: she wouldn't mind the attention. As long as the tumor could be operated on and removed, she wouldn't mind people asking her how she was, and then actually giving a shit about the answer. She wouldn't mind missing a few weeks of work, either. Or, for that matter, a few months . . .

But the doctor does not suggest, as Petra had hoped he would, a brain scan. Instead he sends her home with a printout from the Internet of the maneuver she is supposed to perform while lying on her bed: detailed movements of her head in a certain order, and for a certain length of time, designed to dislodge the crystals from the wrong place they have floated to, if they are indeed there.

Before she leaves the office, the doctor offers to walk her through the maneuver on his examining table. Petra declines, thinking maybe he is some kind of perv, and because from the diagrams on the printout she can't really picture what he's talking about doing to her. Later she finds out that the treatment he's prescribed is pretty standard procedure when a person has what she probably has, and she feels like an idiot.

But she forgets about this when the dizziness goes away after she follows the instructions at home, and for a few days she thinks she's in the clear. Then, on the fourth day, it returns worse than before.

When antibiotics don't help, the doctor agrees, reluctantly, to a scan. Everything comes out fine. She lets him manipulate her on his table, thinking maybe she'd done it wrong at home, but this doesn't help, either. When they seem to have exhausted all of the medical options, the doctor suggests that her vertigo may be psychogenic, which means caused by anxiety or depression or some other condition of her mind. She drops the doctor then and there—not that he knows, not that she tells him this in his office, but the minute she gets home, she starts searching for primary care physicians who are taking new patients, and signs up for a woman close to her own age. This doctor is nice enough, but she can't locate the source of Petra's dizziness, either. Petra leaves the office feeling despair, and resigns herself to just live with it.

At least she *can* live with it—she knows she's relatively lucky, from the stories she's read online about people who can't drive, or even sit as a passenger in anything that moves, without vomiting. People who can't leave their houses, or work at their jobs. Petra can do all of these things. She just can't lie flat or sleep on her left (preferred) side; she needs to avoid bright or flashing lights; and she has trouble at the hairdresser and the dentist, when they want to tilt her back in their chairs. Sometimes, too, the odd movement of her head at a sudden sound or sight will set her off.

It's an inopportune time to suffer from dizziness, and to never know, from one day to the next, how bad it's going to be. Petra's in one of her dating phases, during which she corresponds with men through an online site, then takes the subsequent, progressive steps (if the light appears green on both sides) of phone call, coffee, and dinner. So far this time around, she hasn't gotten to a second dinner, but she keeps telling herself it'll happen, she just needs to keep her head up—or is it down? Well, one shouldn't invoke maxims that refer to the head when suffering from vertigo, anyway—and fate will reward her. It'll be her turn soon, it's about time.

I forgot to mention that Petra isn't exactly young anymore; that's important to know.

One day at work when she is scrolling through the site instead of doing what she's supposed to be doing, a new profile catches her eye. "DWM (Dizzy Wry Male) seeks understanding female companion to share my tilted world." Intrigued, not exactly sure what she might be getting into, and without letting on that her world is tilted, too, Petra agrees to coffee, via the site's chat function, without the intermediate step of a phone conversation.

Gil's waiting for her when she arrives. Though she knows it is shallow and doesn't matter, he's better-looking than she allowed herself to imagine—she figured that, like most people, he'd uploaded a photo that made him appear more attractive than he is—and when he looks up as she approaches, she can tell he's thinking the same thing about her. She gets her coffee and sits down across from him, and they begin to talk. Oh, it's been so long since she had this! The spark of a connection. Excitement. Hope. He started feeling dizzy seven years ago, he tells her, and Petra's shock at the thought that her condition might also last that long is almost entirely obscured by the exhilaration of flirting.

His is a worse case than hers; she recognizes this right away. He tells her he was diagnosed thirteen years ago, on his thirty-fifth birthday, with a vestibular disorder that doesn't respond to the usual treatments. His dizziness is often accompanied by migraines that force him to lie on the couch all day, with the curtains drawn. He sleeps with an emesis basin next to his bed because he sometimes wakes up with sudden and violent nausea. He tends to shy away from social engagements, not because he doesn't enjoy them, but because it's so disappointing for him if the vertigo interrupts or interferes. When he does venture into the company of others for any length of time, he often takes medication, which he calls his "people pills."

He took them before coming to meet her, he tells Petra, then admits that given how they're getting along, he probably didn't have to. "For a long time I fought it—allowing my world to shrink. Until one day I remembered that old saying about quality over quantity. If I can meet the one right person, I thought, it won't matter if there aren't any others. Two people can make a very cozy life together, if they approach it the right way."

Sitting there listening to him, it sounds so good to Petra! She marvels at the irony of it: if she hadn't been suffering from vertigo herself, she would never have clicked on Gil's peculiar profile. How many times has she heard the phrase "blessing in disguise," without really paying attention, without really understanding what it might mean? Now, she understands.

They're exactly the same age, they discover—only three months apart. Gil's had a few love affairs, including one with a woman he married, who asked him for a divorce once it became apparent that his vertigo might be permanent. Petra says, *That's terrible*, but Gil shakes his head. "No, she was a good woman. *Is* a good woman. I can understand it—she married a different person. It's not her fault I became this guy." He points both thumbs back at himself.

"It's not your fault, either." Petra feels her face flush before adding recklessly that she'd never behave that way toward anybody she loved. "For better or for worse," she says, then fears she's gone too far. But Gil looks pleased to hear it. What's *her* romantic history? he asks, and she recites the selective response she's devised over time for just this inquiry:

a few long-term relationships that "ended up not panning out." Gil seems less disturbed by the vagueness of this answer than some other men have. He and Petra finish their coffees and decide to move on, *right then*, to dinner. By the time she gets back home, she's been gone six hours.

To make a long story short—although actually it isn't really all that long at all, it's just that you can probably fill in the blanks yourself, or nearly enough that it doesn't make a difference whether you've got it exactly right—five months after they meet in the coffee shop, Petra and Gil marry, not in some big, nerve-racking affair with attendants and guests, but a simple ceremony in front of a judge. (She has to discard the prototype invitation she designed and printed at work, excited beyond all proportion at the notion of sending them out, but never mind; she knows it's probably true what everyone says, that the wedding isn't the important thing, what matters is the marriage.) She moves into his place and they go about making their cozy life, he continuing to work from home and she at the same job she's had for years, in a cubicle in a building in the city. In bed, they are quite the pair; neither of them can get on top without feeling dizzy, so they find a sideways progression of moves and positions that satisfies them both, even though it precludes variety and improvisation. At night they watch TV, and on weekends they take long walks along the river, which clears both of their heads.

For a few months after they become husband and wife, Gil wakes on some mornings reporting that he feels less dizzy than usual, and while Petra knows she should be glad for him—and she *is* glad, really, on some level—it also gives her a slight chill to the gut, for what reason she chooses not to explore. When, after two weeks of what seems like consistent improvement, he stands up one morning and has to grab for the bedpost, then says he feels worse than ever, she is ashamed to recognize relief in her heart, though Gil himself is less discouraged by the relapse than she expects him to be.

Petra never thought she could be as happy as she believes she feels these days, riding the train out of the city after work and then walking from the station to her new home, where she is greeted by someone who asks about her day, and is glad to see her. Her experience of herself in the world has improved by many, many degrees, almost all the way up to "second to none," a phrase she once heard a coworker use to describe how she felt about her own life. Petra envied the other woman, but never dared to aspire to so exalted a state. Sometimes she feels guilty, now, about loving her life as much as she does—she hasn't always lived up to the standards her mother, or other people for that matter, would have expected of her—but on the other hand, who's keeping score? Maybe God or whoever sees something in her that Petra herself doesn't. Not that she believes in God, but a lot of people do, and what if they're right instead of her?

There's no question of children—both Gil and Petra are too old for that. But they adopt a dog, whom they name Vertigo, or Vertie for short, which amuses Gil more than it does Petra. Though she doesn't realize it at the time, he intends the dog's name to be a point of departure, when they meet new people—as they often do, walking Vertie around the river—from which they can move directly to confessing their joint affliction, their shared vertigo. She understands his instinct: it makes him more comfortable to reveal his vulnerability sooner rather than later (as he did in his dating profile), so that nobody will expect too much of him. Also, he says, it weeds out the people you don't want to waste your time on, if they're going to have a problem with *you* having a problem.

While this makes a certain sense, Petra still asks him to refrain from telling people, especially right away, why their dog has the name he does. The truth is that she can't stand the idea of anyone getting the impression that she's had to settle, though this isn't something she would ever allow herself to know or say. So when Gil asks why, she cries, "They're total strangers! Besides, we're more than that, aren't we? I don't think of it as my identity—being dizzy. It's not the first thing I want people to know."

Gil considers this—it's one of the things she loves most about him, that he listens so closely—and asks, "What *is* the first thing?" But when she can't come up with an answer, he tells her, "I guess I *do* feel like it's my identity, at this point. It's been so long for me now, and it does kind of define my life. You know: I spin, therefore I am." He's trying to make her smile, but this time it doesn't work. Reluctantly, he agrees to stop explaining Vertie's name, at least to people they've only just met.

Gil likes making friends at the river. It's social, but without any commitment; you can leave anytime. They become friendly with Britt and Lucas, two tall Scandinavians whom Gil and Petra refer to privately as The Vikings, in an effort to camouflage their jealousy of the strapping couple who look as if they would be in equal measures shocked and insulted if death or disease ever came for them. The Vikings ask Gil and Petra spontaneously one Saturday if they want to come over for dinner that night. Petra can tell that Gil's about to decline—they have a standard excuse, for the rare occasions they're invited somewhere—but before he can give it, she accepts the couple's offer, ignoring the betrayed expression Gil bores into her. At home, they argue. "We never do anything," Petra says, doing her best to hide the exclamation point in her tone. "We're always cooped up here."

Gil looks stricken. But instead of responding directly, he asks her to call off the date. She reminds him that they were only given an address and a time to show up, not a phone number.

"I can't do it!" he cries, sounding no longer angry, but anguished. Petra resists the temptation to tell him to suck it up. She offers to go to the dinner by herself, but Gil dismisses this option. "I'll manage," he says, like (Petra thinks) the martyr he is, and he takes twice the usual dose of his people pills before they set out.

Britt and Lucas's condo is filled with books, and when Petra asks with a laugh, "You haven't *read* all these, have you?" Britt looks at the shelves, shrugs with a blush, and says, "Well, most of them. Yeah, maybe all." There are also numerous photographs of vacations they've taken together. Many show them in kayaks—it's the Vikings' favorite thing; they've offered to take Petra and Gil out on the river, but Gil's afraid of the waves—and there are also pictures of trips around the world, including one of them at the Great Wall and one in front of the Kremlin. About the last Britt says, "I just had to go to Moscow after reading Chaykovskaya. They have a whole tour you can take of all the settings in the book." When Petra only laughs again, Britt hurries to ask if she and Gil travel much, and Gil says no, he's a terrible flier; Petra can tell he's on the verge of explaining why, but before he can do so, she announces that they don't have a lot of free time (a lie if there ever was one) or any discretionary income (not so much of a lie), but that she hopes they'll have both someday and be able to take some trips.

"I'm actually surprised to hear *you're* not a traveler," Britt tells Petra. "Your name is so . . . international sounding."

Well, that is exactly what Petra always intended when she changed her name from Patty after graduating from high school. It wasn't even an official change—she just began putting *Petra* on her job applications from then on, and it stuck. Her family always insisted on Patty, but there aren't any of them left, so who's to say what her "real" name is?

This isn't something she ever thought worth mentioning

to Gil, though, and he's staring at her with a kind of *what-the-fuck* smile after her comment about hoping they'll be able to travel the world someday. In an effort to deflect the smile and the stare, she tells them all that she's always wanted to see the Sydney Opera House.

The Sydney Opera House! Where does *that* come from? In fact, she has zero interest in either architecture or opera. It's just the first thing that comes to mind when she thinks of Australia, which is the first place she thinks of that's faraway. When she says it, Gil laughs outright. Lucas and Britt look at each other as if they'd had a bet going between them—whether it was a good or a bad idea to invite these two for dinner—and they've just realized who won.

The evening ends early. They never see Britt or Lucas again, because they take to walking Vertie (sometimes together, but more often separately now) in a different direction altogether, away from the river on the commercial, less scenic route.

What finally puts an end to it all (I say this so matter-of-factly because I'm sure you can see it coming, though you will probably be wrong about the how and the who) is Petra's growing awareness, shortly after their third anniversary, that she isn't dizzy anymore. She's grown so accustomed to it—the low-level imbalance, the subtle, almost unconscious adjustments she's learned to make, accommodating the tilt and veer—that when it leaves, it takes her a few days to notice. At first, she doesn't trust that it's gone, and she tests herself, cautiously, by lying flat on her back for an hour, by subjecting herself to the strobe lights at the teenagers' stores at the mall. When neither of these brings on vertigo, she drops into a hair salon, asks for a wash, and lets the girl tilt her head in the sink at an angle that would have produced agony not long ago. Nothing. She emerges with her old sense of balance, and a new style of hair.

What is it that's caused her to recover? She has, of course, no idea. And what does it *mean* to recover—that she's gotten her old self back? She has little if any desire to recall what her "old self" was.

It takes her a few more days to tell Gil, who, once he hears what she has to say, sits without blinking for almost longer than Petra can bear. Just as she's about to explode from the rage of it, he gets up from his chair to come to her, then cradles her head between his hands before kissing the top of it with a tenderness she hadn't seen coming. He says slowly, "Well, maybe this is good timing. I've been thinking that maybe we've run our course."

"What?" It doesn't sink in right away. "Wait a minute— *you're* dumping *me*?" The absurdity of this makes her laugh, which, she can see, only confirms for her husband the truth of what had seemed hard for him to say.

"Whatever we had once, we don't have anymore." His smile is sad, with something else in it she can't or would rather not place. He's talking about the vertigo—right? She feels dismay seep through her, at the idea that they had been bonded by so thin and pathetic a paste.

But there'd been more to it than just that! She knew there had been. They'd discovered a lot of things they had in common, both before they got married and after. They loved each other—right? The dizziness had only been the occasion of their original meeting. It was the context, the backdrop, not the *reason* they'd decided to join in this cozy life.

Gil shrugs in the way she found so endearing, the first time they met. Even then, after only a few hours, she recognized that the casual motion was for him *not* casual, but rather an acknowledgment of how important a thing had just passed between them. That day, he'd shrugged after asking if she wanted to stay where they were for another coffee, or head up the street for a meal. *As long as you're sitting across from me*, he'd said to her, *I don't care where the table is.*

Today, the shrug signals the end of their marriage. Petra looks away, thinking she might have to run for the vomit pail, she feels so blindsided and so ill.

Whatever happened to "for better or for worse"? Gil had told her he didn't require that line in their vows, but Petra insisted. Had she thought, in some remote part of herself she rarely accessed, that by committing herself to a man who was so compromised, she'd become a different person? More generous, more appealing... someone she herself might admire, if she met herself out in the world? Someone who might actually visit the Sydney Opera House, or give a shit about her job, or love a decent person the way he deserves to be loved?

Though he's sitting very close to her, he has receded from her sight. She shakes her head with as much force as she can muster, willing the world to spin. "Don't do that, honey," Gil says, wincing. "You're hurting yourself! You'll bring it all on again."

But her luck's run out—she understands that, if nothing more. No matter what she does or how hard she might try, she'll never be able to get it back.

CLIFF WALK

"This is the most stunning place I've ever been to," she told him. "I'd love to get married here."

Stuart didn't know what to say. Did she want to get married to *him*, or did she just mean married in general? He decided to play it safe. "I know. It's something."

"They're so lucky," Valerie added. "The weather, this day—how'd Cecile get so lucky?" She seemed to believe he might actually have an answer to this.

Stuart shrugged. "Positive thinking?"

She laughed. "That's a good one. Cecile's the least positive person I know."

"Well, she's *your* friend," he reminded her, annoyed by her laughter. "Don't ask me."

Luckily, she didn't pursue it. "Can you believe this view?" she asked, gesturing about them with the light shawl draped loosely across her shoulders.

"It's something," he repeated, though he knew this was not as effusive an agreement as she was looking for. He had trouble speaking superlatives; they always sounded insincere and pretentious coming out of his mouth. Words like *gorgeous* and *spectacular*—he avoided these. "It's unbelievable," he tried out, and felt relieved when all Valerie did was nod in response.

"Someday," she murmured, looking out over the water, and he knew better than to ask what she was referring to.

They stood above Narragansett Bay. Around them the cliffs and mansions of Newport rose into the bluest of summer skies. It was after the wedding, and guests scattered all over the wide lawn, talking or clumped together on the dance floor next to the string quartet. That morning, clouds had made the bride nervous, but by noon, they'd cleared out and taken the wind with them. Earlier Stuart could have sworn that Valerie had been hoping for rain, but of course he would never have told her what he suspected. Cecile was not exactly Valerie's friend, but her boss on the staff of the alumni magazine for a college neither of them had attended. Valerie's salary as assistant editor augmented what she made selling the short stories she wrote. She published two or three a year in a famous magazine that paid well, where she received good exposure and made a name for herself. Someday soon, the stories would be collected into a book. Stuart figured that when this happened, she would move on from him. She'd be invited to parties and flown down to New York, and she'd meet new people more interesting than some guy she'd struck up a conversation with while they were both waiting for take-out Chinese.

This was how Stuart thought of himself, as "some guy." He tried not to let on to Valerie, because he knew insecurity was unappealing. He tried to act confident, but at times she saw right through him. He could tell when this happened because she got a look in her eyes that he read as, *I can do better*. She never said anything, though, and in fact, it was at moments like these that she acted the tenderest toward him.

But the end was coming. He felt it the way you feel a cold coming on, the perversely delicious anticipation of the suffering you are about to endure.

They moved back up the hill toward the party, where Cecile was getting ready to toss the bouquet. The best man invited all the single women to come to the front, and Valerie muttered, "What the hell," and went forward with mostly younger women and little girls. Cecile took clear aim at her niece, who couldn't have been more than eight. But just as the flowers sailed, Valerie stepped in front of the child and caught them in both hands. The niece began to cry, and around him Stuart saw people frowning at Valerie and murmuring disapproval. He cleared his throat in embarrassment and tried to smile as Valerie rejoined him.

"I don't know what came over me," she whispered fiercely. She seemed aware of the discord she had created, but not how to fix it. "It was like, if I didn't catch those flowers, something bad was going to happen."

"To Cecile and Martin?"

"No. To *me*. It was like a flash of obsession or something—you know, those people who have to say the Lord's Prayer fourteen times before they get out of bed in the morning? Or skip stairs or count syllables in their head?" She handed him the bouquet, though he said, "*I* don't want it," and she moved to the line at the bar, where he watched her wait alone as other guests turned to chat with one another. He knew he should go over and stand with her, but instead he went back to their table and put the bouquet on her chair. They left the reception soon after, without the prize she had stolen, and Valerie was silent on the way back to the inn.

Neither of them felt hungry for dinner, but they'd asked the innkeeper to make reservations for them, so they felt obliged to go. The restaurant was a walkable distance, but Valerie wanted to take the car. "My feet are killing me from those heels," she told him. "Please, honey, can we drive?" His heart knocked against itself when he heard her say the word *honey*. Whenever she called him that, it inevitably and inexplicably followed that they had a fight.

It didn't start right away. They had time to kill before their reservation, so they idled in front of shops around Thames Street. In the bookstore window, Stuart pointed to the new collection of stories by the Russian author he'd been reading the night he and Valerie met in the Chinese restaurant. The book, which Stuart had found in the library, was what Valerie had noticed first. "Do you like her?" she'd asked him, and it took Stuart a moment to realize she meant the book's author.

"I do," he told her. "It's different. I don't usually read this kind of thing, I prefer realism, but she makes it *feel* real. There's this one about a talking sugar bowl—"

"I know," Valerie interrupted. Then she seemed to realize this sounded rude, so she apologized and went on to explain that she herself was a writer. When she mentioned the magazine in which her stories had appeared, he felt a hot stone of jealousy lodge in his own chest. He'd never had anything published, but Valerie assured him that someday he would. Her encouragement was what kept him coming back to his legal pad in the early mornings, before he left for his job as a programmer.

He wrote stories, too, but not the same kind as Valerie. Hers tended toward the dark and sad; they were internal explorations of people nobody would look at twice on the street, or suspect to have the depths she discovered in them. Or were those depths she *created*? He knew it was the second, though it felt like the first. Her characters were not generous or relaxed or optimistic, but you understood that they wished more than anything to be all of these, and more; Valerie wanted you to understand that they couldn't figure out how to get out of their own way to see the path. These were characters you might not necessarily like, or want to have as friends, but the way Valerie wrote about the problems they faced and the pain they suffered, you got at least a glimpse into *why* they said the wrong thing, behaved badly, or sabotaged themselves. You understood them more than if they were real people you came across at the office or on an airplane or in a checkout line.

In his own work, he set out to celebrate the more positive side of life: people doing the right thing, even if nobody else knew it; feelings of inspiration, admiration, hope, and—most of all—love. Valerie had read his stories, and though she didn't say so, he knew she considered them too simple, too idealistic. One of his favorites, very brief, was about the life-long bond between a young boy and a man who could have been, but was not, his father. Their connection is so strong that when the boy becomes a man and things go wrong in his life, so wrong that he contemplates suicide, the memory of the man—and of himself as a child—is enough to save him. Valerie used the word *sentimental* about the story, and at first Stuart thought it was a compliment. Then he realized that *sentimental* was about the worst thing you could call a piece of fiction these days.

"I wish I saw the world the way you do," she told him. "I really do."

"I'm not sure we *see* it any differently. I know all that bad stuff exists. I know you're writing about real things. The difference is what we choose to focus on, that's all."

"'That's all'? But that's everything," she said.

Now, in front of the Newport bookstore, he offered to buy Chaykovskaya's new collection for Valerie, but she declined. He hesitated before asking, "Do you mind if I buy it for myself?"

"Of course not. Why would I mind?"

Why, indeed? He wouldn't have been able to say, except that he was accustomed to being so careful around Valerie, depending on her mood. They went into the store, and she browsed in the sections farthest from fiction—Crossword Puzzles, House and Home—while he made his purchases, including a second book he hadn't been looking for but decided spontaneously to buy when he saw it on a table next to a sign that said *Unsought Gems*. On the way to the car to drop the bag off, he said, "You're not going to read it? The Chaykovskaya?"

"I will eventually." She sighed and reached for his hand. The touch thrilled him, so much so that he almost missed what she said next: "I'm ashamed to admit how jealous I am of her. That's petty, right? And childish. And a waste of time."

It was so rare of her to confide in him that he felt almost suspicious, then ashamed of that feeling. "No. I think it's perfectly natural," he said. "It's fair to say she's become a sensation." When she remained silent, he edged his toe closer to what felt like more dangerous water. "Do you think it's because of what she does with magic? Making you think a story's set in reality, then subverting it somehow, like with the sugar bowl?"

Valerie paused, and for a moment he worried he might have said the stupidest thing yet. So he was relieved when she told him, "I know I'm in the minority, but to me her stories *are* realistic. I think the sugar bowl isn't actually doing that talking—that's a fantasy. It's just what the housewife hears in her head."

"Oh." Should he try to convince her otherwise? He was sure (like most of the reviewers he'd read) that it was otherwise.

"And that's to her credit," Valerie added. "It means the stories don't rely on a fantastic premise or exotic settings. She's interested in the psychology of her characters more than anything else." She let go of his hand as they began to walk toward the restaurant. "She's basically doing the same thing I do. Which is why I'm jealous. She does it so much better."

Should he try to argue this? Tricky call. He decided arguing wouldn't end well, and he tried instead to distract her, pointing out the gorgeous view of the bay as they were led to their table, but she barely looked. The server came over with a plate of sliced tomatoes, a basket of rolls, a cruet of oil, and a small tray filled with white circles. Compliments of the chef, he told them.

Stuart mused aloud about what the white circles might

be. Valerie raised her eyebrows to show it was a silly question. "Mozzarella," she told him, as if educating a child. She spooned one onto a tomato slice and lifted it to her mouth. "Mm, try it," she said.

He followed her example and swallowed, but something seemed off, and then he realized what it was. "Does that taste like cheese to you?" he said, pointing to what they both now understood were round pats of butter for their rolls. Surreptitiously, Valerie spit out the rest of the tomato mix into her napkin.

"Goddammit," she said.

Stuart tried, but found it impossible to keep from laughing. "Do you *mind*," Valerie said, as people from the next table looked over and smiled at his mirth.

"I'm sorry, honey," he said, hoping his use of the endearment would mitigate her desire to find fault with him. "But don't you think that's hilarious? You can dress us up, but . . ." He nodded toward the chef's treat now lying desecrated on the plate between them.

"Speak for yourself," Valerie said. She stood and walked out of the restaurant. Stuart let her get a head start, as if she'd just gone to the ladies' room; then he reached into his wallet for cash, which he left on the table, got up, and, slowly so as not to attract attention, followed her out to the car.

He found her pulling desperately on the locked passenger door. "Valerie. Honey," he said, putting the key into the lock. "It's been a long day. Let's just head back and go to bed."

"I feel like such an idiot," she said.

"Because of the butter? Anyone could make that mistake."

"No, not because of the *butter*." She spit the word as if it were the last thing she wanted to have in her mouth. "Because of the way I acted with the bouquet."

"But you had an urge," he reminded her. "A sudden impulse,

a scare. You thought something bad would happen—"

"—if I didn't catch it. I know." She motioned for him to start the car. "But I should have been able to control myself. I mean, did I really believe that anything actually depended on whether I caught a bunch of flowers somebody tossed through the air? How stupid is that?"

"It's not stupid. Superstitious, maybe, but not—"

"And I stole it straight out from under a child! In front of everyone. Oh, I can't stand myself." She pushed her forehead into her hands as they pulled up at the inn. She made no move to get out, so Stuart didn't, either. They sat in the warm dark, listening to noise emanating from the bar down the street.

Finally he said, "You felt genuine fear back then. When the bouquet got tossed."

She made a noise he could not interpret.

"And you reacted, without thinking. It's nothing to be ashamed of."

Valerie inhaled deeply. He thought she was going to thank him for being so patient with her, so understanding, but instead she said, "Could you please just stop talking? If we have to say one more word about it, I'll scream."

This took him aback, her vehemence. How quickly hatred for herself could turn into hatred for him. Casting blindly for a subject less likely to irritate her, he asked, "Do you still want to go on the Cliff Walk tomorrow?" The innkeeper had told them about one of Newport's foremost attractions, a path next to the bay that wound by many of the old-money mansions.

"Oh, I don't know," Valerie said. "Do we have to plan everything? Let's just see how we feel when we get up." Finally, she opened the car door and stepped out.

"*I'd* like to see it," Stuart said, but she was already at the top of the steps waiting for him to take out the room key, and he knew she hadn't heard him.

*   *   *

In bed, everything was quiet—the sex, and the murmured exchange after it, before sleep. Always, Stuart felt genuine affection in Valerie's touch, and he did his best to remember this when they *weren't* touching and when he felt he was boring her, or when he sensed that no matter what he said or did at any given moment, it would not be enough to dislodge whatever already occupied her attention and her thoughts. As he tried to find a comfortable position on the pillow, the name of an old girlfriend came to him suddenly, and he wondered what had happened to her. Then Valerie threw her arm across his chest, and, feeling guilty, he stroked it until she made noises of contentment and fell asleep.

In the morning he woke at six—his usual time—and waited for Valerie, who usually slept for an hour longer. On the nightstand beside him, the bag from the bookstore contained the gift he'd bought for her when she wasn't looking. She still hadn't begun stirring by seven thirty, and he remained quiet on his side of the bed, waiting for the right moment to place the book on her pillow.

She was a light sleeper, so he tried not to rise before she was awake. It meant that he had time, every morning after they'd spent the night together, to think; sometimes he didn't have an hour's worth of things to think about, but luckily today wasn't one of those days. He remembered the wedding and the reception and the abbreviated dinner of the evening before, and he thought about Valerie's compulsion to catch the bouquet. It was something they had in common, he realized only now. He'd had moments like that, when he felt that something had to be a particular way or the consequences might be dire. Once he'd been on a road trip with an old girlfriend—the one he'd thought about the previous night—and as they were about to enter the Burger King in a rest area, he had a sudden bad feeling about what might happen if they went through the restaurant's front doors. Instead he took the girlfriend's elbow and steered her around to the side. The whole time they were eating their Whoppers, she looked at him as if he were crazy, and she ended their relationship soon after that.

It *was* a kind of crazy, Stuart supposed, but that didn't mean the feelings weren't real. Who could say that a bus wouldn't have come crashing in through the plate glass at that moment, if he had ignored his instinct and just gone through the front? So he understood why Valerie had stepped forward to catch the bouquet. For all she knew, she might not be alive this morning if she hadn't.

They got up together and put on T-shirts and shorts; the weather called for a sunny day, with the temperature near eighty. Valerie was in a much better mood. She seemed touched by the book he'd bought her, a very old edition of Yeats's collected poems, and she seemed to have forgotten that she'd been iffy about the trip to the Cliff Walk. She said she was excited that they were on their way. Stuart warned himself not to get his hopes up, but he couldn't help it; ever since she'd shown him the *Save the Date* from the bride and groom, he'd imagined this weekend moving him and Valerie to a new realm of intimacy, in which they might also decide to commit to a life together.

In high spirits they ate breakfast at the inn, then headed out for the day. "I could set a story in this town," Valerie said as they made their way along the charming streets.

"What would it be about?" He was always afraid he was asking dumb questions when they talked about writing, even though he still aspired to become a writer himself.

"Oh, I don't know yet," Valerie said. "Maybe a wedding on a cliff. Maybe a woman who goes with her boyfriend to a beautiful restaurant next to the ocean, but all she can think about is how stupid she is for not recognizing butter when she sees it." She smiled, and he realized she meant him to understand that she was mocking herself.

The Valerie who wrote her stories—about people who were ordinary and vulnerable, and in such ways that Stuart found it easy to inhabit them all, including ornery grandmothers and faithless spouses and people whose moral behavior left something to be desired—was the woman he loved, and the one he sometimes found it hard to locate in the woman who seemed so often to have little use for him. The real Valerie, he believed, was the one who excavated those troubled fictional souls, because she understood and sympathized with the state of wishing to be a different kind of person but failing to know how. Like many of her characters, she was, in the end, *kind*, Stuart thought.

But you wouldn't have known this by just talking to her. For some reason, the face and demeanor she presented to the world did not match what she was inside. He felt sure about this, but had no idea how to express to her how much better it would be for everyone—herself included, herself *first*— if in real life (to use a phrase she'd told him she considered redundant) she could not only show but *be* who she really was.

It had something to do with the snatching of the bouquet, her insistence on hiding. Didn't it? With the fear of being stripped as bare as the characters she conceived of and then exposed. If she took control—even in ways that felt a little *out* of control—it meant she could manipulate what other people discovered about her, and keep the rest safe to herself.

Wasn't he right? He felt that if he could understand it, he could help her undo it, because surely she must wish it to be undone. And if he was wrong, he didn't want to find out, because it meant that the Valerie who wrote those sensitive stories was the false one.

It was still early, only a little after nine, as they strolled down Narragansett Avenue. People were already jogging or strolling along the Walk. Stuart and Valerie got out of the car and approached a sign that said *Forty Steps.*

From the brochure they'd been given at the inn, he read aloud the paragraph describing the way servants from nearby mansions used to gather at this stone staircase, during Newport's golden age, to dance and play the Irish music that reminded them of home.

"This says it's especially dramatic just after a storm," he continued, "when the waves crash into the rocks." He turned to Valerie. "Want to go down?"

She shrugged. "If there'd just been a storm, maybe. But it doesn't look like much now. Forty steps? Big deal. Let's just keep walking. This way looks nice." She started off toward the right.

"Wait. Wait." Stuart was aware of encroaching panic, though he knew that revealing this to Valerie would be a mistake. "Please, honey? Can we just go down once and see what's there?"

"I really don't want to," she said. "Stuart? Come on, let's go."

But he couldn't make himself move from where he was standing. There was too much at stake. "Just do me this favor," he said quietly. "Please?"

But she would not do so, even though he could tell she understood what was making him beg her. She enjoyed denying him this; he could see that, too. As she started walking along the cliff by herself, he thought about running after her and confessing. *If we don't do this, something bad will happen.* And he knew what it would be.

But she had already moved on ahead of him. She picked up a little stone and threw it into the water, where it drowned without making a sound.

BEQUEST

The woman her husband had married after he left her was the last person Jean expected to hear from. When the phone rang, she did not even look at the caller's number because she figured it would be her daughter and her grandchildren, calling to wish her a happy birthday. She was buttering an English muffin and boiling an egg, treating herself to a hot breakfast. Today she turned sixty-three, a fact that seemed impossible, a fact that scared her. She did her best to ignore it herself, but she wouldn't object to her family celebrating her.

Outside, it was already eighty degrees. Her pool had been open for a week now and she had not gone in yet this season, but maybe today was the day. Her grandchildren thought she must be rich to have a swimming pool in her backyard, but that was because they lived in the Northeast, where such a thing might be true. She had explained to them that, in Arizona, a lot of people owned pools. The children, a boy of eleven and a girl of nine, had only been here once, a few years ago, but it was at Christmastime and the pool had been closed. Her daughter kept saying she would bring them during a summer, but so far it hadn't happened because the kids had camp, tennis lessons, and friends. Usually, Jean went back East to visit *them*.

Picking up the phone, Jean looked forward to hearing her grandson's voice—still sweet and high, not yet coarsened by hormones—saying, *Happy Birthday, Grandma,* with an affection she assumed he would tire of revealing someday soon, but which she intended to relish in the meantime. So when instead there was a pause before the other person spoke, Jean almost hung up. But then came the woman's question: "Have I reached Jean?"

"Yes," Jean said. "What is it?" She felt annoyed and disappointed that it wasn't her grandson. She didn't want her egg or her muffin to get cold. She didn't feel like talking to a stranger.

"This is—Patsy." The woman's hesitation implied that the name would mean something to Jean, but it didn't.

"Patsy who?" Then, of course, she realized—and as she did, she couldn't help taking in a breath, and she cursed herself because she knew the other woman had heard it.

"I'm sorry to call like this. I know this is out of the blue." There it was, that slight Southern accent Jean remembered from the tennis courts when they all lived outside Chicago and used to play mixed doubles, round-robin-style, at the town park on summer Saturday nights. Patsy had been the only one who ever came to play without a male partner, so the other women took turns sitting out. *Cheeky*, they said about her behind her back, but they all—Jean included—admired her audacity; she wanted to play tennis, and she didn't let the fact that she was single stand in her way. They had all come of age on the pages of Gloria Steinem and Betty Friedan. They understood that Patsy behaved as they themselves would aspire to, if fate had not granted them husbands. That she possessed a stronger backhand than any of them, and the courage to poach balls at the net, also kept them less catty than they otherwise might have been. They accepted her into their circle—a confidante to the women, a cheerleader to the men—and when she left to return to Florida, it was with one of their own.

It was Jean's turn to say something, but she couldn't fathom what it should be. Perhaps sensing this, Patsy continued. "I don't know if Merry would have told you. That I was sick?" Patsy's backyard near Pensacola bordered a pretty marsh; Jean's daughter had shown her photographs the first time she came back, as a teenager, from visiting her father in his new home. Jean wondered if Patsy was looking out over birds in the water, as she was, at the same moment, watching a cardinal skim across the surface of her pool.

"I don't call her Merry, but yes, she did mention it." It was a few weeks ago, during their usual Sunday phone conversation, routinely initiated by Jean after she got home from church and before one or both of Meredith's kids went to play on some kind of team. *Look, I know you don't like to hear about her*, Meredith began, *but she* is *a part of my family and I think you should know.* She had never been skilled at tolerating conflict, and when she tried to muster defiance, she sounded as if she might cry. Which softened Jean's heart a little, even in the face of her resentment at Meredith's referring to Patsy as "family." *She has cancer*, Meredith said. *It's bad, in the bones.* When Jean didn't say anything, Meredith faltered, repeating herself: *I just thought you should know.*

"I'm sorry to hear that," Jean had told her daughter finally, though she was not sorry, not at all. Later, after hanging up, she asked herself a question not unfamiliar to her: What kind of a person *am* I? And within an hour, she'd managed to put it out of her mind. Meredith had not mentioned it since then. So this morning, with Patsy calling to tell her she was sick, it was as if Jean were hearing it for the first time.

"I know you're going to think this is crazy," Patsy said, and Jean did not feel the apprehension these words might have evoked, because with an uncharacteristic surge of prescience, she knew what the other woman was going to say. "But I was wondering if there was any way we could see each other before—" She interrupted herself to start a different sentence. "I thought you might want to come and pick out something of Walter's."

"Did you know today was my birthday?" Jean realized this was an odd response, but it had occurred to her suddenly that Patsy may have been keeping track of Jean's life in some way, for some reason, since stealing her husband, or maybe only since burying him three years ago next to her own parents in a cemetery on a bluff overlooking the gulf. Jean had not gone to Walter's funeral, but she imagined the quadruple plot laid out under palm trees, waiting for the fourth stone.

"Um—what? No. Well, Happy Birthday." Patsy sounded farther away now, and Jean wondered if she was taking pills to smooth out the pain.

The cardinal was back, pecking at the top of the pool. It seemed not to understand the concept of water, of something not solid under its feet. "Anyway, you can't be serious," Jean said into the receiver, and this time she was the one who heard the breath pulled in quick on the other end. "You're the last person I want to see."

"I can't believe you said that to her," Meredith told Jean on the phone the next day. She'd called her mother on a Friday rather than waiting until the weekend, which was how Jean knew her daughter felt it was important.

"I can't believe she *told* you I said it." It had gotten warmer outside, but she still hadn't tested the pool. She wasn't quite sure what she was waiting for. She knew that swimming alone was a risk—you heard it all the time—and yet it had never bothered her before. Maybe it was her recent birthday; maybe she was, it occurred to her, losing faith in her ability to save herself.

"Why shouldn't she? It bothered her. It made her feel bad."

"She should have thought of that when she waltzed off with your father."

"That's not how it happened, and you know it." Meredith spoke with such conviction that Jean wondered what her ex-husband and Patsy had been telling her all those years. She didn't want to fight with her daughter, but she felt she had something to preserve, here: her own self-respect, and the way her only child thought about her.

"I think I know a little more about it than you do." She tried not to sound condescending, but wasn't sure she succeeded. "I mean, really, Meredith, you were thirteen."

"That's old enough," her daughter said calmly. "To know what was going on."

What was going on? It wasn't that Jean didn't recall yelling at Walter, and him yelling back at her—about big things, little things, so many nicks along the beam running from the absurd to the critical. She remembered it all too well, and yet there was also something missing about that time, when she thought of it now. She couldn't quite identify what it was, the vapor or poison that had seeped into their marriage when neither of them was looking, a toxin without a scent. Though she couldn't have labeled it, she recalled the distinct and unacceptable sensation that she, and not Walter, was its source.

Not anger exactly, and not anger only. But it was easier to feel anger than fear or sadness, and easier to turn it against Walter than herself. From this distance she found it hard to reconcile all she'd felt, back then, with the simultaneous and comforting vision of those Saturday nights at the park, the tennis courts alive under yellow lights, the pleasure of everyone's confident agility as they distracted themselves from the obligations of jobs and bills and children, anticipating the drinks and camaraderie they'd share afterward at The Gold Crown in the center of town.

They had been winners then, all of them, and not just on the court. They were young, with houses and families they believed no one could take from them, and people hadn't started getting sick yet, let alone dying. *Invincible*, Jean thought now; that was the right word. She was only beginning to understand how dangerous it had been to feel that way.

On the phone to Meredith, she said, "I suppose she also told you that I said what I did in response to *her* saying she wanted to see me?"

She could tell from the surprised silence that, in fact, this was news to her daughter. "What about?" Meredith asked.

"She said she wanted to give me something of Daddy's." The childish word slipped out from habit before she could revise it. "But I'm guessing there's something more. What it could be, though, I have no idea."

She did have some idea. Patsy wanted to apologize, no doubt. But Jean didn't voice this suspicion to Meredith, who had excused herself to speak to Jean's granddaughter.

"Sorry," Meredith said, coming back on. "Somebody said something mean to her on the bus today. I never have this kind of thing with Jake. What is it with girls?"

"They start early," Jean said, "and it never ends. Wait until she grows up." She almost laughed, remembering the outraged contortions of her daughter's little face as she described the latest injustice committed by her best friend. But she refrained at the last minute, realizing it might irk Meredith, and returned to the original subject. "Anyway, I don't think I'll be flying to Florida anytime soon, thank you. Can you imagine? Her and me in a room together?" She was pretty sure this wasn't grammatically correct, so she hastened to pile on more words. "Not exactly my idea of a good time."

Another pause, and she knew Meredith was thinking. She also knew better than to prompt her daughter; ever since childhood, Meredith had bristled against being expected to say anything before she had figured out what it was she wanted to express. It used to drive Jean crazy, though Walter always implored her to be patient. "We're lucky she isn't one of those people who just likes to hear herself talk," he said, and Jean tried to agree with him. On the phone, though, it was difficult to wait until Meredith was ready. Finally, with the receiver hot against her ear, Jean could stand it no longer. "Are we done, honey?" she said, and on the other end Meredith made the clicking noise with her tongue that meant she didn't want to be hurried.

"Not yet." Jean pictured her daughter standing in her split-level in upstate New York, surrounded by the paraphernalia of her family's daily life. Though years ago the idea would have made her laugh, the truth was that Jean missed this—having people to keep track of, rooms getting messy faster than she could pick them up. For a moment, before her daughter spoke, she felt intensely sorry for herself. Then Meredith's next words wiped the feeling away. "I can imagine how hard this must be for you," she said to her mother. "What if I went, too?"

It was complex, what followed—the series of emotions Jean felt when the sentence registered. One was excitement at the prospect of seeing Meredith; another was jealousy that her daughter would make such a trip to see her stepmother, when she'd told Jean she couldn't see getting away for a visit to Arizona "in the near future."

But more than either of these, she felt—what was it, exactly? Not quite dread at the idea of coming face-to-face with Patsy again, but apprehension. Before she could think about how it would sound, she asked her daughter, "Why would I want to do that?" knowing intuitively that Meredith understood the real question: *What's in it for me?*

"Mom." Now her daughter's tone was chiding, as if it were her own child she spoke to instead of her mother. "Like I said, I know it's hard. But the woman's dying."

"Well, I'll be dying someday, too. Just because she's doing it first doesn't . . ." But there was no remotely advisable way to complete this sentence. Already she could see that she was going to have to make this trip, not because she felt she owed it to the woman who'd married her husband, but because her daughter would hold it against her if she failed to grant Patsy's wish. It wasn't fair, of course, but very little was, she'd learned, when it came to what adult children expected of their parents.

"Just a sec," Meredith said suddenly, before Jean could give her answer. "Ophelia's having a meltdown. I'll call you right back."

Jean replaced the receiver slowly, after holding its heat to her cheek. Nine years later, she was still getting used to having a granddaughter with such a conspicuous name; she herself was *Jean* precisely because her own mother had held such a distaste for what she called "showing off," in any form.

She picked up a pencil and jotted a list of things that would need taking care of while she was gone. *Plants. Pool. Mail.* It wouldn't be any more than an overnight, right? How long could it take, whatever it was that this woman wanted from her?

Outside, the reading on the thermometer slid above ninety. Peering through the window, she saw what she thought was a dead bird on the far side of the patio, then realized it was only a clump of mud left over from the rain of the night before. Relief hit her so hard that she had to sit down. She was still sitting ten minutes later when the phone rang again, and reluctantly she began to make plans for a journey she would not have chosen to take.

At the airport, Meredith rushed to greet her, late to the gate, apologizing; she'd been picking up the rental car, she said. But Jean knew from the smell of her daughter's breath that although she may indeed have picked up the car, she had then stopped in at one of the terminal bars for a glass of wine, or maybe even two—her plane from Rochester had landed an hour before Jean's own.

She felt annoyed by this, but wouldn't say so. Now she'd have to be the one driving on unfamiliar roads. Besides, what did Meredith feel she needed fortification for? She wasn't the one who should feel nervous about seeing Patsy. She and Patsy got along. Patsy was part of Meredith's family— Meredith had said so herself. The thought of it chilled Jean's skin, but at least it wouldn't be that way for too much longer. When Patsy died, that would be it. Walter was already gone; once Patsy was out of the picture, Jean could pretend that their marriage had never existed, if she wanted to. She could pretend that she was, in fact, a widow. It wouldn't be that much of a stretch, because everyone she knew in Arizona believed this anyway.

Their return flights were early the next morning and they'd made a hotel reservation for the night. They decided to check in after the visit because it was already one o'clock by the time they met at the airport, and Patsy had told them she did better—had more energy—during the days than in the evenings. "Do you have directions to the hospital?" Jean asked once they'd reached the highway.

"We're not going to the hospital." Meredith turned to give her a puzzled look. "We're going to their house." When she saw Jean's reaction, she let her voice get away from her, as she had done all her life when she felt wronged. "Mom, I told you that!"

"I don't think you did," Jean murmured, though it was true that she had not written down everything Meredith said in their final phone conversation the day before. "I thought she was dying," she added, to divert Meredith's pique.

"Well, *eventually*." Meredith clicked and looked out at

the palms lining the highway, which made Jean feel all the more that she was in a foreign place. "But she might still have weeks yet."

"I thought she was on her deathbed, more or less." Jean was surprised at the relief she felt to learn this was not the case; she had been imagining an awkward scene in which a pale Patsy with matchstick arms—the same arms that used to send those crosscourt backhands over the net with such force—groped at her to beg forgiveness, before flopping limp and weakened onto the bed. And because the other woman was so frail, Jean would have to feel guilty when, no matter what she managed to say for the sake of decorum, she still hated her.

"I don't think so. She has caregivers coming in, but I don't think it's to the point of hospice yet."

Jean wanted to ask how Meredith knew this, but before she allowed herself to do so, she realized that it might prompt an answer she wasn't prepared to hear. Had Meredith *seen* Patsy recently? Had she kept secret from Jean another, earlier trip to Florida? How dare she?

Meredith seemed to understand what her mother was wondering. "She sent us some pictures a few weeks ago. Some friends of hers threw her a party when she finished chemo. She didn't look too bad."

"Does she still wear her hair in that silly way?"

"You mean long?"

"Yes, I mean long. Long hair looks silly on a woman her age."

"Actually, Mom, she's *lost* her hair." Meredith didn't even need to adopt a shaming tone; the words contained their own rebuke. Jean let the comment sit between them for a moment or two, recognizing that her daughter would want to savor it, before reaching to turn on the radio. They listened without speaking until they reached Marsh View Drive, where Meredith directed Jean to pull into the lot of the convenience store on the corner.

"I think we should stop here and use the bathroom. I don't want to be rude by having to pee the minute I get there."

Rude. It was all Jean could do to purse her lips, nod, and follow Meredith into the store. When they came out of the restroom, Meredith caught sight of a stuffed-animal bin. "Maybe I should get the kids some souvenirs," she murmured, fingering an orange platypus.

This was too much; Jean couldn't hold it in. "You mean like *My mom went to visit the woman who broke up her family, and all I got was this lousy T-shirt?*"

Meredith's fingers froze in the animal's fur. "Forget it," she said, then started walking toward the exit without looking back to see if her mother was coming, too. They both slammed their doors getting into the car, and Meredith gave terse directions to Patsy's address. Jean tried to imagine Walter living here, and couldn't. And yet he had. Happily, from all reports. She wondered where the cemetery was— likely, not too far. Would there be any point in visiting his grave site? Probably not, since she hadn't attended his funeral or, in the last five years of his life, talked to or seen him except when he'd called to say how sorry he was to learn that her mother had died. Speaking to him then, it had been all Jean could do not to start crying on the phone. She'd hung up too soon, then started to call him back before commanding herself, out loud, to stop.

She parked in front of the house Meredith indicated, then had to bend over the steering wheel to catch her breath. "What's the matter now?" Meredith asked, as if Jean were feigning something. When she saw that it was real, she reached to put her hand behind her mother's back. "It's okay, it's okay, Mom. We're not in a hurry. Take all the time you need."

Did she feel guilty for having been mean to her mother?

Jean could not be sure, but Meredith went on to describe the plan: a caregiver was scheduled to arrive at six, to prepare dinner for Patsy and spend the night. It was a long trip they'd made for a short visit, but Jean felt relieved to hear it would only be a matter of hours. Maybe, after she and Meredith said good-bye, they could find a nice restaurant somewhere, then fall asleep watching a movie together in their hotel room. It had been years since Jean had slept with someone she loved in the same room. She looked forward to it.

Her daughter's solicitude had the opposite effect of what Meredith intended. Instead of calming Jean down, it irritated her. She did not like being vulnerable, let alone having someone else witness it. She stepped out of the car and squared her shoulders.

"Let's do this," she said. She thought it might have been a line she'd heard in a movie once, from soldiers or a SWAT team.

She let Meredith walk up to the stoop first. Patsy came to the door after the bell had been rung twice, and she hurried them inside more quickly than Jean would have liked; she nearly tripped on Meredith's heels. "Sorry, sorry," Patsy said, shutting the door behind her guests before Jean had completely cleared the entryway. "The cars go by so fast on Marsh View, and I'm a little paranoid about the cat getting out."

The cat? Walter had been allergic, the last Jean knew. She herself had never been an animal person, had never understood why you would want to have animals in your house, but there was no benefit, as she'd found out on a few occasions, to admitting this.

She looked away when her daughter hugged Patsy, then stepped forward herself with a huge, unnameable swelling in her chest. Her husband's second wife stood before her, hands at her sides, looking as if she wanted to offer a bigger smile than she did but was unsure whether it might backfire.

Meredith had been misled, Jean saw, or maybe she just hadn't wanted to believe the truth, which was that her stepmother was closer to death than Meredith could allow herself to acknowledge.

"Jean," Patsy said. "You made it. It's so good of you to come. "With a labored inhalation, she added, "When was the last time?"

"I don't know," Jean told her, but like so many other things, this was not true: she was perfectly aware that the last time had been New Year's Eve, 1992—or more precisely, the first hours of 1993—at a party thrown by someone in their tennis group. Later that spring, just after the nets had been put up again for the season on the park courts, Patsy moved back to Florida, where she'd grown up. A few months after that, Walter followed.

More than twenty years—closer to twenty-five. No, closer to thirty! Other than the gaunt pull to her face, Patsy looked to Jean almost exactly the same as she had back then, except instead of long hair (which she used to tie back for tennis), she wore a scarf on her head. Even as Jean hoped Patsy would think she hadn't changed, either, she knew it wasn't the case—her face carried the deep lines that had begun appearing during the divorce, and since she'd had to stop playing tennis because of her knee problems, she'd gained more weight than she cared to keep track of.

But of course, Patsy didn't mention any of this as she led them into the living room. Meredith said, "You switched the furniture around. I like it." She took a seat at one end of the couch while Patsy lowered herself onto the other. There was a matching love seat that looked comfortable, but this Jean ignored, opting instead for one of the two accent chairs. The coffee table was spread with what Jean would have called *appetizers*, but which Meredith and Patsy referred to as *tapas*. At the end of the table stood bottles of wine and seltzer; Meredith poured herself a glass of merlot, while the two other women chose water. Leaning back to drink, trying to relax, Jean looked around at the modern décor and marveled again at the notion that Walter could have felt at home here. She'd always thought of him as preferring a more traditional style, but either she'd been wrong about that, or he'd changed along the way.

On the mantel sat a dish containing a piece of rose quartz in the rough shape of a pyramid. About this, Jean did not inquire as she might have in someone else's home, because she remembered at the last moment something Meredith told her once after returning from a visit: she'd gone to bed with a bad headache, and Patsy had moved the dish into her bedroom, saying the crystal would help her heal. Jean scoffed at the story, though Meredith took pains to tell her that when she woke up, the headache was gone.

Next to the dish was a framed photograph of Walter and Patsy with Meredith when she was in high school, wearing a sundress Jean had never seen and a Miami Dolphins cap, also unfamiliar. Anyone who didn't know better would have thought it was a picture of Meredith with her parents.

"I appreciate your both being here," Patsy said after a silence so awkward—so literally breathtaking—that it occurred to Jean to stand up and announce that she was calling a taxi, because this was all just too much. "I always thought I'd be the one who'd go in a car crash—I'm a really bad driver, do you remember that, Jean?—and Walter would be the one with the slow death, some disease." She shook her head and smiled, as if amused. "It just goes to show."

"Dad would have made a terrible patient," Meredith said. To Jean's consternation, she was already reaching to top off her glass. She felt like telling her daughter to slow down, but she didn't want to embarrass Meredith, and—more— she didn't want to come off as a shrewish mother in front of Patsy, who was no doubt much more tolerant, and cool, than Jean ever was. "Remember that time he thought he had pneumonia, Mom? He made you drive him to urgent care, and insisted on them taking an X-ray, and when they told him it wasn't pneumonia, just a bad cold, he said they must have mixed up his X-ray with somebody else's?" She gave a sloppy snigger and wiped a tear from each eye.

"Oh, I know," Patsy said, smiling. "He was like that with me, too. If I had a headache, he worried it was a brain tumor. Indigestion: a heart attack. He was the worst." The smile bloomed into a full laugh as she looked out the window at the marsh edging the backyard, as if she thought Walter might be out there, lifting his hand in a wave.

Jean did not recall the urgent-care visit Meredith had described, but her dismay over this evaporated when she heard Patsy's story, which triggered a memory of the time she'd been whacked in the eye by a tennis ball, playing at net. Walter was about to serve, three courts over, when he saw that Jean was crouching, her hands to her face. He sprinted over to her so fast—weaving around net posts, jumping over racquet bags—that later someone said it had been like watching O. J. Simpson running through the airport in the Hertz TV ad. Because her eyes were covered, Jean had smelled her husband before she saw him—she recognized his sweat. Inhaling it, she'd relaxed, even though her eye throbbed, her vision wavered, and she was scared.

On the way home from the hospital, bandaged and suffering a headache, she thanked him. "You have nothing to thank me for," he'd said, looking sideways at her in surprise. "Don't you know that? If you get hurt, we both do."

Now, she wished she had remembered this line when he'd told her he was leaving her—and not only leaving her, but going to Patsy. *If I get hurt, we both do, remember?* she would have liked to have said, but it hadn't occurred to her at the time.

Despite this bitter thought, Jean also recognized the impulse to thank Patsy for reminding her of the comfort she'd taken that day in her husband's—*their* husband's?— words; for reminding her of how close she and Walter had been then; and of the fact (one she forgot all too often these days) that she had been loved. She didn't know how to go about conveying such an oblique gratitude, though, so instead she asked Patsy about her illness, the treatments, side effects, and whether she had any family in the area.

At the last question, Patsy shook her head. "No, it's just Merry now"—she smiled at Meredith, who smiled back as she reached again, blurrily, for the wine bottle—"and, of course, Fidel."

"Excuse me?" Jean said.

"Our cat."

The first reference had been to *the* cat. This time, it was *ours*. Jean did not have to ask where the cat's name had come from. It would have been Walter's idea of a joke.

"I'll get him!" Meredith shot up suddenly, bumping her shin against the table in the process. She swore, rubbing her leg, and limped away from them down the hallway.

Jean asked, "How does she know where he is?"

"Well, he always sleeps in the same place. The night I came home from the police station after Walter died, I found him curled up on a pile of Walter's T-shirts on our closet floor. It was like he knew somehow. That sixth sense cats have. I've left the shirts there for him ever since." She paused, and Jean tried but failed not to make a face at the idea of shirts that had been lying around unlaundered for three years. "We got him when he was a kitten, but he's really old now, so all he ever does is sleep." They waited for Meredith to appear with the cat, Jean filling her mouth with stuffed olives so she wouldn't have to talk. When Meredith still hadn't come back after several minutes, Patsy eased herself to a stand—

watching, it was hard for Jean to imagine that this diminished woman was the same one who used to ace men with her serve—and began walking slowly in the same direction Meredith had taken.

When she returned, she had a different kind of smile on her face—amused, but also (it pierced Jean to acknowledge) maternal. "She fell asleep," she told Jean in a low voice. Gesturing at the wine bottle, she added, "I don't think she's used to drinking so much. This whole thing must be stressful for her."

"She's not on the closet floor with the cat, I hope," Jean said. She did not want to talk with Patsy about her daughter's stress.

"No. They're both on her bed. She's doing that rubbing thing with her finger on the side of her nose."

"She's been doing that since she was a baby," Jean said, stabbed by the sudden memory of watching her infant daughter asleep in her crib.

Patsy sat down again slowly and adjusted her scarf, which had started to slide down on one side. "Listen, Jean, I'm just as glad. Really. It's you I wanted to talk to."

Jean had the impulse to call for her drunken daughter to wake up and come back to join them. But she could also feel an underused muscle inside her psyche wanting to flex itself, so she resisted calling for rescue. Though she understood that she was on the verge of something she had not anticipated, she could not yet tell whether it would be welcome or not, and she trembled down to her wrists.

"Is it hot in here?" she said abruptly without quite planning it, pushing up her sleeves.

"Oh, I'm sorry. Usually I'd have the AC on. But it makes me too cold now. Are you very uncomfortable?"

"Not at all," Jean said, though she was. She stood and walked across the room to the bookshelf, where she pointed to a title and said, "Hey, I read that one. The talking sugar bowl, right?"

"Oh, the Chaykovskaya?" Too late, Patsy appeared to realize that pronouncing the author's name so fluidly might be perceived as showing off. "Did you like it?"

Jean shrugged. She hadn't actually *read* the book, only taken it out of the library because the cover had drawn her eye. "It was okay. I'm not really a fantasy fan."

"Oh, I loved it." Patsy seemed to draw fresh energy from the fount of her own enthusiasm. "You don't really have to think of it as fantasy, if you don't want to—I took it as more of a metaphor than anything else."

"Well, anyway." They had entered another territory in which Jean did not feel secure. She sat back down and said, "Go ahead."

Patsy leaned forward. "Okay. I've been having some phone sessions with this fellow who helps people die. A coach, kind of," she began, and Jean burst out laughing. When Patsy looked taken aback, she said, "I'm sorry. It was the word *coach*. I just had this image of some guy with a whistle screaming 'You can do it!' in somebody's ear just before they—well, you know." Even as she spoke, she wanted to take back the words, but really—it was too much.

Patsy had recovered herself. "I know what you think of my beliefs," she said quietly. "I know you think I'm a kook."

"I wouldn't use that word," Jean said, though, in fact, it was the exact word she had used about Patsy to Meredith more than once.

"I know your spirituality is more—traditional. Sometimes I wish mine could be, too."

Jean tried not to let show, in her face or in the way she shifted across her seat, the guilt that Patsy's words evoked in her. When she'd moved to Arizona, she'd thought about not going to the trouble of finding a new church, but ended up picking one because she knew that this was what her mother would have expected of her. She went most Sundays, but it was more out of habit than anything else.

"Walter felt that way about it, too. Jealous. He wished he could have faith in something." Then Patsy blushed, as if worried she had offended Jean. "But you already know that."

She didn't, though. And she didn't understand why Patsy would mock her now, why she would spend the energy to summon Jean across the country just to make fun of her, when she needed all her reserves to fight for her own life.

"He did *not* feel that way," Jean told Patsy. "Why would you say a thing like that?" Though only a moment ago she had vowed to respond charitably—because all along, she'd assumed an effort at atonement might be forthcoming—she heard herself deliver these words with defensive scorn. "He thought only idiots believed in God. We almost didn't get married over it." The minute she'd made this confession, she regretted doing so.

"That may have been true once," Patsy conceded. "But you didn't know him, later on. He told me he wished he could convince himself something was out there. He said he didn't feel as if what was here was enough." There was no hurt or rancor in Patsy's voice. She took as deep a breath as she seemed to be able to manage, to help her get the next words out. "Anyway, this coach—his name is Sanjit, though I got him to admit it used to be Brad—says we should all take care of unfinished business if we can. That's what I'm trying to do here."

Jean prepared herself to hear remorse. She had already decided that she would tell Patsy she forgave her, even though it would probably not be the case.

"If you have something to say to me," she told Patsy, in what she hoped was a magnanimous tone, "I'm ready to hear it."

Her premonition (only days before had she found the

courage to identify it as, instead, her hope) was this: Walter and Patsy had had a fight on the day he died, shortly before he peeled out of the driveway and, turning onto the main road from Marsh View Drive, miscalculated the speed of the van heading toward him. What they'd been arguing about: Walter had realized, after all these years, that he'd been right the first time—it was Jean he'd always wanted to be with, not Patsy, and if Jean would take him back, he would go.

Patsy would tell her this, after which she would say she was sorry for her part in it all. Jean could see and hear it so clearly that it was almost as if it had already happened. Across from her, Patsy shifted and gave a small smile. What did *that* mean—the smile? "Is there something in particular," Patsy said, "that *you* want to hear from *me*?"

Enough of this! Were they going to tiptoe around it the whole time? Jean had made a long trip at her own expense, she might as well say what was on her mind. Patsy was literally asking for it. "Well, okay. I guess I'd like to hear how you've been able to live with yourself, all these years." Her heart quickened. Was that because she was starting a confrontation, or because she was starting one with a dying woman? The quizzical expression on Patsy's face exasperated her. "After stealing my husband."

This time it was Patsy who laughed, bending forward to clutch a sofa cushion to her side. "You make it sound as if Walter was an umbrella you set down in a restaurant, and I picked it up and walked off with it at the end of the night. Oh, my God. For some reason that strikes me as funny. I haven't laughed in so long. And, Jesus, I might not ever again. So I guess I thank you for that."

"I wasn't trying to be funny." Jean stood up. Where did she think she was going to go? "And I don't expect to hear an apology from you. But you asked, so I answered." When had her voice taken on that holier-than-thou tone she used to despise in her mother's? And how much would it cost her to switch to an earlier flight?

"Wait a minute," Patsy said, lifting herself from among the cushions. "You're serious? You actually believe that's what happened—that I 'stole' him from you?"

"Well, how would *you* put it? We were perfectly fine until you showed up. The next thing I knew, my husband became *your* husband."

"The next thing you knew! That's a good one." Patsy gave her ghost-smile again, though it turned into a wince when something invisible passed through her. "So now Walter has gone from being an umbrella to a puppy, distracted by the newest shiny thing. Do you hear what you sound like, Jean? Talking about him as if he couldn't help himself, at every step of the way. As if he didn't make his own decisions. And did it ever occur to you that you weren't in fact 'perfectly fine,' even before I came along?"

"That's just what you tell yourself," Jean said, trying to keep her voice from shaking, "to justify what you did." *The newest shiny thing* was exactly what Patsy had been back then, she realized. They had all been distracted, mesmerized, by the glitter she brought to their lives. She sat again, but this time on the very edge of the seat. "Why did you really ask me to come here?"

Well, I know it must seem like a letdown now, after all this"—Patsy gestured at the heat in the air between them— "but I really did want to give you the chance to take something of Walter's, if you want it. The house is going to be cleaned out when . . . soon . . . and I'm in purging mode." She struggled to readjust herself against the couch cushions.

"Oh." Now Jean heard her own voice as an echo, reverberating through these rooms foreign only to her. "Why would I want something of his? Whatever he was going to give me, I got a long time ago."

"Well, then, fine. I thought I was doing something nice." This time, Patsy did not hold back her yawn. "But I don't care, Jean. I've got other things on my mind right now, besides your investment in being a victim."

Her investment in being a victim! The nerve!

"Wait. I'm sorry. I shouldn't have said that." Patsy made a beckoning motion, as if trying to call back her words. "I was lashing out just then, and Sanjit says it's a waste of my energy, at this point, to spend it on anything other than being kind. I'm supposed to be focusing on that as my mantra: *Be kind, be kind, be kind.* I try. But after a while, it's just non-sense sounds in my head." Jean watched as the other woman appeared to struggle with herself. Then she spoke quietly, as if half hoping she wouldn't be heard. "Look, Jean, it hurts me to tell you this. But Walter would have preferred to work things out with you."

Jean snorted. "I suppose he told you that?"

"Yes." Patsy looked pained. "He did. It didn't mean he didn't love me, but I asked him once, and you know him, he was always honest, even when you didn't want him to be." With the fingers on one hand, she dug into the other palm, and Jean wondered if she was trying to mitigate her psychic distress with this measure of physical pain. "If I weren't in the position I'm in now, I doubt I'd ever admit that to you. But I am. In this position. And there's no reason you shouldn't know the truth."

Lowering her tone to match Patsy's, Jean said, "He could have made it work out anytime he wanted. He's the one who left, do I need to remind you?"

"He thought that's what you wanted."

"What *I* wanted?" It was delirium on Patsy's part, she thought. She'd read about such things happening to people who were dying. "Why would I want that?" But then she was afraid of actually hearing an answer, so she foiled Patsy's chance to give one. "You said you wanted me to take some-thing of his?" The sooner she did what this woman asked of her, the sooner she could get out of here.

"Oh. Yes." Patsy's face brightened, as if she shared Jean's relief at the change of subject. "When you said you'd come out, I put a bunch of his things in the guest room. On a card table. Don't get your hopes up—it's not like there's all that much to choose from, and nothing valuable. I thought you might want something from his office, or a piece of his cloth-ing. Don't worry, I won't offer you one of the T-shirts Fidel sleeps on." She smiled and closed her eyes, and it was a few moments before she was able to open them again. "You're not going to strangle me in my sleep, are you?"

"Of course not," Jean said. "With my daughter right down the hall?"

They both smiled then, this time at each other. For a moment they were the old Jean and the old Patsy—or, it made Jean feel better to think, they were the *young* versions of themselves, friends exchanging volleys at the net or, side-lined together out of the round-robin, trading confidences on the grass beside the courts. What had those confidences contained? Jean's would not have been about her marriage; of that she was sure. She and Walter had made a pact early on that whatever was between them would always remain there.

But obviously he had violated that pact, hadn't he? It would not have been possible for him to leave her for Patsy without doing so. For her part, Patsy had wanted children, Jean remembered now. She remembered Patsy telling her how lucky she was.

And she remembered thinking, when Patsy said this, that she and Walter had fooled Patsy, and probably everyone else.

What? A false memory—it had to be. Jean dismissed it, then watched with fascination as even in the middle of trying to form and say something further, Patsy dozed off, her head dropping to her shoulder. She hugged the pillows supporting her, then gave in completely to sleep, her features relaxing for the first time since Jean and Meredith had arrived an hour before.

Jean walked quietly down the hall, looking first into the wrong bedroom—the one Walter and Patsy must have shared, which contained a hospital bed now—and shut the door, so she wouldn't make that mistake again.

In the next room she found her daughter asleep on a bed with the cat stretched across her feet. Though Patsy had referred to it as "the guest room," Jean saw that this was where Meredith had stayed when she came to visit; the wallpaper was nearly identical to that of the room she occupied in the house Walter and Jean, and then Jean alone, had raised her in, and a poster of Alanis Morrissette still hung on the wall, faded and curled with age.

The card table Patsy had mentioned was set against the window. Jean approached it warily, both curious and apprehensive about what she would see. A tennis racket leaned against one of the legs, but not the one Walter had used all those years ago, the steel model Jimmy Connors had made famous; *that*, Jean would have liked to have had. She thought of the way men wore their shorts so short back then—what had they all, as a sport, as a society, been thinking?—and it made her smile.

Some old concert programs. A watch with a black band she didn't recognize. The blotter from his desk at work, the leather one Jean had given him when he got his first promotion, just after Meredith was born. She touched it and remembered, but did not pick it up.

A glass paperweight enclosing a pressed flower—definitely not Walter's style, or at least the style Jean had known him by. A humidor containing cigars, which she did not know he'd smoked. Patsy had been right: there wasn't much. Or more likely, there were other things somewhere, but the items before her were the ones Patsy was willing to let go.

She didn't want any of this crap, and she felt annoyed, anew, by Patsy's arrogance. She'd asked Jean to come all this way—put Jean through this—so she could feel better about herself on her deathbed knowing that the first wife had claimed a desk blotter?

She was about to turn from the room without selecting anything when, among several loose items in a shoebox, she caught sight of an old billfold, which she didn't recognize at first. When she did, she had to stifle a cry as she picked it up—*He saved this*—as she rummaged to find a faded pair of old train-ticket stubs. New York to Boston, an April morning in 1980, after the weekend she'd accompanied Walter to Manhattan when his new company sent him down to meet the people from other branches he would be working with. Jean had never been to New York, and during the days she walked miles, going into stores without buying anything, eating pretzels from street vendors, sitting on a bench in Central Park holding a book on her lap but not opening it because there was so much around her to see. She remembered thinking, *I can't believe this is my life. How did I get so lucky?* Riding Amtrak back to Boston, she sat next to the window, and as it hurtled past stations in New York and Connecticut and Rhode Island, she put her hand over her heart, feeling the need to contain something as people outside turned to wave at the passing train. When she called Walter's attention to it, he leaned close to notice the tears in her eyes, and asked why she was crying.

"I just love the fact that people still wave at trains," Jean told him. "I can't help it. It just makes me happy."

He reached to take her hand and squeezed it. "That's why I love *you*," he whispered, putting his mouth close to her ear. "Reason eight hundred and seventy-six." Two months later,

Jean learned she was pregnant, and they were convinced that the child had been conceived during that magical weekend. Jean thought that no one deserved to be as happy as she felt then, and immediately she found herself waiting for the bad news to come, for the other shoe to drop. She had almost stopped waiting when Patsy moved into their lives.

Standing in the bedroom listening to the soft sounds of her grown daughter—a mother herself now—sleeping, Jean closed her eyes and had to lean against the wall to hold herself up. When had it happened? When had she stopped being the kind of person who cried at the sight of people waving at passing trains? She did not know, except that with her hands closed hot around the old ticket stubs, she understood for the first time that it had taken place before Walter left, not after. Not *because* he left.

She also understood the real reason Patsy had asked her to make this trip, the real gift she wanted to bestow: the lie that Walter would have liked to remain married to her. It had to be a lie—didn't it? Jean supposed she should appreciate this impulse of generosity on Patsy's part, but she couldn't quite manage appreciation, when what she actually felt was even more inferior and petty because, as much as she believed she wished to, she did not possess such generosity herself.

And, oh, be careful what you wish for! Had that ever been more true? Patsy had given her the very thing she thought she'd wanted. But having gotten it, she couldn't reject it fast enough.

When she left the room, Fidel plopped down from the bed and followed her. Silently she shooed him up the hall before her, in the direction of his sleeping mistress. Back in the living room, the cat seemed to consider jumping up to join Patsy, who was still asleep against the couch cushions. But he thought better of it and took Jean's chair instead.

What kind of visit was this, with the other two people

asleep? For all that talk beforehand about how limited it would be, they weren't exactly packing in the quality time. But she had to admit it was kind of comforting; no need for decorum or pretense, when death was in the house.

She went over to the window and looked out at the marsh just in time to see a cormorant swoop down. Quietly she moved to the back door, opening first the inside and then the outer screened one, before stepping onto the stoop. She felt and saw a flash by her feet and in the next moment realized it was Fidel, rushing past her to streak across the yard toward the bird now spreading its wings as if to announce, *I'm here, come get me!*

"Fidel!" she whispered fiercely, already understanding how pointless it was. The cat came to an abrupt halt when it reached the water, and the cormorant flapped a further taunt. Fidel ran down the length of the backyard, apparently seeking a bridge to the marsh, but when this didn't work, he turned and sprinted back in Jean's direction.

For a moment, she dared to believe he was returning, and her stomach unclenched in relief. "Good boy, good boy," she told him. But instead of stopping at the house, the cat darted around to the front. Jean hurried to follow, but by the time she reached the driveway, where she'd parked the rental car, she could only barely see Fidel bounding up Marsh View Drive.

Jean tried to swallow what was in her throat, but it wouldn't dissolve. She turned to see Patsy in the doorway, watching with a hand over her mouth. Then Meredith appeared behind her stepmother, pushing by to explode onto the lawn. "What did you *do?*" she cried at Jean. She had the rental keys in her hand and tried to pull the car door open, then dropped the keys in the grass.

"No way are you getting into that car," Jean told her. "Give me those. I'll go."

From the house, she could hear Patsy's wobbly voice saying, "Jean, you don't have to do that," but this was far worse than if she'd let loose a torrent of vitriol. Jean drove slowly up the street and found herself praying she'd see Fidel, despite understanding that even if she did, she had no way of luring him back. They were not familiars; why should he come to her?

At the corner she pulled into the convenience store lot. Inside, the attendant recognized her from their earlier bathroom stop and said, "Come back for this guy?" as he picked the orange platypus out of the bin. Jean shook her head and asked him if he'd spotted a black cat. "Jesus, I hope not," he said, trying again to make her smile until he realized it was a lost cause. Back in the car she sat for twenty minutes, stalling and trying to feel some relief from the AC, but relief was not something her mind or body would make available to her.

When she finally worked up the courage to return, another car was in the driveway and for a moment she thought she'd pulled up to the wrong house, but then she saw her daughter in the doorway, giving a quick thumbs-up. Hardly daring to believe what she thought it must mean, Jean went in to find the caregiver helping Patsy settle into her hospital bed, Fidel panting on a pillow beside her. "Oh, thank God," Jean murmured.

"I knew he'd come back," Patsy said. It was taking her more time now to summon the breath she required to speak. "Nobody would be that cruel."

Jean wondered if by *nobody* she was referring to the cat or God. But she wasn't about to ask, besides which the caregiver told them quietly that it was probably time. "No," Meredith said, her voice containing a pitch of panic Jean hadn't heard in years, "I don't want to." But they had all, including her, known it would come to this, and in the next moment she stepped forward bravely and wrapped her stepmother in a careful but ardent embrace. Jean and the caregiver stepped into the hall to give them a few minutes in private, and Jean was just as glad she couldn't hear what they were saying; though she suspected it was selfish, she couldn't help thinking of this as a rehearsal for the scene she and Meredith might have to enact someday.

Meredith came out of the room with her hair hanging in her face, but Jean could still see the tears. She thanked the caregiver and told Jean she'd wait for her in the car. Jean resisted the intense urge to just follow her out of the house and be done with the whole thing, but she knew she had an obligation, so with a freshly hammering heart, she entered the room and leaned over to kiss Patsy's cheek. It smelled of powder and lemons, not death, though before that moment, Jean hadn't remembered she knew what death smelled like.

"Good-bye," Patsy said, giving her old sly smile. "Goodbye. Look it up, Jean, will you? It might surprise you."

Look *what* up? But she was hardly about to ask the dying woman to clarify. Probably it was a conversation Patsy thought they'd been having, or one she was hearing in her head. The drugs could do that, Jean knew. She took one last look at her old friend—no, at her husband's second wife—no, at her old friend—then held her breath and went outside to join her daughter, who had sobered up and insisted on driving to the hotel.

Not too many minutes passed before Jean intuited that it was anger rather than grief keeping Meredith silent. "What's the matter?" she asked because there seemed no choice, though really whatever was the matter, right now, was the last thing she wanted to hear.

Meredith inhaled deeply, then let the breath out too fast and coughed. "Do you think I didn't hear you out there? The way you were talking to her—the things you said?"

It seemed like days rather than hours ago. "You *couldn't*

have heard us," she told Meredith. "You were asleep."

"I was pretending."

"Well, if you did hear us, then you know about the things *she* said to *me*."

"That's different. She's sick." Meredith turned onto the highway that would lead them to the hotel. "Besides, she was only responding. You started it. And what about the cat, for God's sake? Do you know what a shit show that could have been? How could you let him out when you knew how afraid Patsy was of that *exact* thing?"

Jean pressed her window open an inch to get some air. "I'm sorry about that. I do feel bad. But that's what cats do, right? It wasn't really my fault."

Meredith slapped the steering wheel with both hands. "Of course it was your fault, Mom! If it wasn't *your* fault, then whose fault was it?"

"Nobody's. Not everything has to be somebody's fault." Yet even as she spoke, Jean understood there were questions she'd never be able to answer. Had she let the cat out, or had he escaped? Or had she let him escape? Had there been an instant in which she recognized he was there behind her, poised to spring, when she could have shut the door and kept him inside where he belonged?

And the last in this series of questions, not for the first time: What kind of person *am* I?

It would not bear considering. "Do you want to go out for a nice dinner, honey?" she asked. "My treat?"

But Meredith only looked at her sideways before slowly shaking her head. They should just grab some takeout, she told her mother, and go to bed. The next morning at the airport, her hug was rigid and brief. "Talk to you soon, Mom," she said before entering her boarding line, and despite how hard Jean willed her to, she did not turn back to wave or to blow a kiss.

Sitting in her own terminal, she replayed yesterday's

visit over and over in her mind, not because she wanted to, but because she had the distinct feeling that it was part of a test she could not risk failing. *Look it up, will you?* was the last thing Patsy had said. On her phone, Jean Googled "cat escape" and "hospice" and even "death," but nothing came up that jibed with Patsy's claim that it might surprise her. Could Patsy have been baiting her, giving an assignment she knew would be impossible to decipher?

No. That would be a waste of her steadily shrinking time. More likely it had all made sense in Patsy's drug-muddled mind, and it just didn't translate to a language Jean understood. Nevertheless, she closed her eyes, focusing as hard as she could on that final exchange. Moments before her seating group was called, she launched one last search and found what Patsy had wanted her to.

"Good-bye," she'd said to Jean, making a point of repeating the word so commonplace it disappears before you even hear it. "Good-bye." It was a contraction, Jean read on her phone screen, of the phrase people uttered centuries ago, when they parted company: *God be with ye.* Back then chances were good that you might not ever see a person again, so you took your leave with a formal wish for each other's health and safekeeping.

Well, *this*—finally—had to be the dig she'd been waiting for. Didn't it? Patsy, with her crystals and her death coach, sending Jean off with a benediction from the divine?

Yet even as she did her best to conclude this, she knew it didn't make sense. Whatever kind of person would do a thing like that, Patsy wasn't that kind of person.

As she watched first neighborhoods, then roads and trees, then the entire planet fall away from her, she wondered if what Patsy had led her to was the truth. But by the time they approached home, she'd come to her senses. She knew perfectly well what *good-bye* signified—she'd understood it all her life. Nice try, she thought as she landed, feeling her lips twist in something other than a smile. How much of a fool would she have to be, to even consider that it might mean not *I am leaving,* but *I love you and wish you well*?

MAN OF COURAGE

It had not been Stephen's idea to swing by his grandmother's, a fact which in later years would cause him to feel ashamed. But once it occurred to his mother, there was no turning back. "You just told me yourself that you didn't have a specific plan," she said as she wrapped the freshly cut brownies in a high tinfoil square, the top of which she then pressed to secure a seal.

Stephen said, "That doesn't mean I was asking you to make me one." When she paused in her task to look at him, he added, "To make one for *us*." He did not return the look but shifted in order to give himself a better view of the driveway. He cleared his throat and wiped his hand on the side of his ironed khakis.

"Well, excuse me if I interfered." His mother didn't move from where she stood behind the counter. Though it had been two years since the kitchen's renovation, Stephen's father still got a kick out of having learned from the designer that this structure was called a *peninsula*. "Our own private Florida," he never seemed to tire of saying, running his fingertips across the smooth faux granite. Or he would tell them he was getting up from the couch for a quick trip to the Balkans, anybody want anything?

"I didn't say you were interfering." At the sound of a car slowing in front of the house, Stephen took a sharp step forward to peer through the door; then his shoulders relaxed. "Nope, that's not her. Mom, I get it. And if it was just me, you know I would. But I'm guessing it's not exactly her idea of a good time, starting off our weekend getaway with a visit to my grandma."

He had continued to avoid his mother's eyes as he spoke, still standing guard at the doorway. But when she didn't respond, he turned, pitched himself toward the peninsula, and said, "Okay. I'm sorry. Forget I just said all that."

She reached out to fix his collar, then went upstairs. His father came down and rubbed at a spot that didn't exist on the countertop. "So you really like this person, I guess?" he said to his son.

"Yeah. I really do." Stephen took a half-perch on one of the stools. "She has a ton of friends, they're all nice. I probably spend more time at their dorm than my own apartment." His mouth moved in what might have been an indication that he was second-guessing himself. "I mean, sometimes she can seem a certain way, but I don't think that's the way she actually is."

"And what way is that?"

"I don't know. Never mind—I don't know what I'm talking about."

After a moment his father said, "I don't suppose you want anything from me in the way of advice or anything, do you?" and Stephen blushed and also looked at the invisible spot and said, "No, no, but thanks, Dad."

When Hayleigh arrived, his mother came back downstairs to be introduced. After the two younger people had left, she said to her husband, "I don't see it, do you? All these years, in all my imagining, I never pictured him with someone like her."

Stephen's father said, "But that's a good thing, right? It obviously boosts his confidence, being with her. We like that, don't we?" He lifted an apple from the fruit bowl.

Stephen's mother clucked. "'You have a smart son here,' she tells me. As if I didn't know."

"It sounds like she started noticing him after he won that physics competition. Not sure what her own major is, but not physics. Anyway, I think she's good for him." He tossed the apple up before catching it with a smack inside his palm. "She's certainly attractive," he added, taking a bite and holding it out to his wife, who declined by shaking her head.

"As if that counts for anything," she said, but she didn't sound convinced.

A half hour after they got on the road, Hayleigh began peeling the foil to unseal the brownies. Stephen said, "They might not taste like what you're expecting. She puts peanut butter in them, that's how I liked them as a kid."

"That's so sweet," she said, taking a bite. "Oh, you're right. They're not like regular brownies." She put the half-eaten square back on top of the pile and closed the foil seal partway before tossing the package into the back seat.

It would take three hours to drive to the lakeside resort where he'd made their reservation. Stephen asked if she wanted to play a game, like *Who Am I?* or *Would You Rather*, but Hayleigh reminded him that she'd made a playlist especially for this road trip, didn't he want to hear it? She plugged her phone into the speakers before he could answer, then proceeded to sing every lyric that came on for the next half hour. Each time a new song started, she exclaimed, "Oh, I *love* this one!" and turned the volume up a notch. At the end of the hour he suggested stopping for a break, and when they returned to the car, he switched the dial down and said he kind of had a headache; would she mind if they just talked for a while?

She noted that they were going to be early—they couldn't check in until three o'clock. "Well, here's the thing," he said, adjusting his hands on the wheel. "Would you mind if we took a little detour along the way?"

"A detour?" She turned to him with wide eyes and an

expression of dawning delight. She poked his arm. "You sneak. You planned *another* surprise?"

"Oh, no. No, no, no, it's nothing like that." He made a sound like the start of strangulation in his throat. "I wish it was, but no. I was just wondering how you'd feel about stopping off for a few minutes—half an hour, max—at my grandmother's. I wouldn't ask, but my mother kind of made me promise. We're going to be so close to where she lives— you know how it is. Then we can go straight to the place and check in, and do whatever you want; you can call all the shots, until we check out on Sunday."

She had turned back to look ahead through the windshield after the word *grandmother*. She shrugged. "I guess. I mean, if you want to. Sounds like we don't have a choice. Is her house near the water?"

"Kind of. You can't see it from the windows or anything. But she's about ten minutes from the beach. My cousins and I used to ride our bikes there all the time in the summer—it was pretty great."

"That sounds nice," Hayleigh said, checking her text messages. "Hey, Zach wants to know if you plan on tracking down any dark matter this weekend. If we see any black holes, he wants us to take some pictures." She gave a snicker-snort. "Doofus. He has no idea what he's talking about—he just looked up 'Physics' on Wikipedia."

Stephen shifted behind the wheel. A few moments passed, and then he asked, "Did you go on a lot of vacations when you were a kid?"

At the question, she paused her thumb in mid-scroll. She laid the phone on her bare thigh and turned to show him a shy-looking smile. "You know what? I love that you just asked me that. Ninety-nine guys out of a hundred wouldn't have asked me that." She coughed a little before continuing. "The only time I remember us ever going to the beach was a trip we took up to Maine the summer I got my period. Oh, that's so cute—I never saw anybody blush as fast as you do!" She gave his shoulder another poke. "Anyway, I didn't know how to plan for it yet—shark week—and I ended up getting it one night right before bed."

When she paused in the telling, Stephen said, in a tone that suggested he wasn't sure whether to ask or not, "Shark week?"

"That's what we called it. It's pretty gross, be glad you don't have to deal with it." She flipped down the visor mirror to inspect her face before continuing. "Anyway, it was raining, we were staying in this crappy hotel with a stick-shift rental car, which was all the place had when we got there, and since my mother doesn't know how to drive a shift, my father had to go out and buy me some maxi pads. This is how mature my father is: he pitched a fit about having to do it, but he went out and got the stuff and came back and threw the bag at me on the bed, then went out to the motel bar to get drunk. Yeah, one of my favorite memories. So no, my family was never too big on vacations."

After a moment, Stephen said, "I'm sorry."

"It's okay, don't be. I like hearing about other people's awesome childhoods. So: you and your cousins? Bikes to the beach?"

"Yeah. It wasn't really all that big a deal." He waved a hand as if to erase what he'd told her previously.

"You don't have to say that on my account. It makes me happy that you had good summers when you were a kid."

Without looking at her, Stephen reached over to touch her hand on the seat beside him. He thanked her for being willing to make the quick stop. "She'll be glad to see us."

"Well. She'll be glad to see *you*." She allowed her hand to linger in his for a few seconds before removing it back to her lap.

When they reached the house, he pulled into the gravel drive behind his grandmother's Honda. "Whoa. She still drives?" Hayleigh asked.

"Yeah."

"I freak out whenever I see an old person driving. I'm, like, whoa, stay away." She made a cross with her fingers and held it in front of her face as if banishing vampires.

"They probably feel the same way about you when they see you texting and turning left at the same time."

"I don't do that."

"You don't?"

"I hardly ever do that. Like you've never sent a text when you were driving."

"I never have."

"Oh, I forgot who I was talking to. Saint Stephen." But she smiled saying it.

They stepped up to the door, Hayleigh hanging behind his shoulder. At the last minute, Stephen paused. "Shoot. I probably should have called or something. She's not all that laid-back, maybe just dropping in like this isn't the best idea."

"Well, too late now." Hayleigh gave a few sharp raps on the door.

It took her a while to answer. "She's probably asleep," Hayleigh said before they heard movement through the house in their direction. "Old people sleep a lot."

The woman who opened the door smiled when she saw Stephen and said his name, then noticed Hayleigh and raised a hand to her own white, slightly disheveled hair. Stephen introduced them. "I'm sorry if we woke you up," Hayleigh said, following him inside.

"Woke me up?" She appeared puzzled by the suggestion. "I was just out back in the garden, pulling some weeds. I wanted to get them up before the rain came." She raised her hands to show the dirt embedded under her nails. "I was about to sit down with my book. I was so excited when it came in at the library, there were so many holds before it came to me. Doesn't that always make you feel good, when a lot of people want to read the same book? Not to mention that this one's short stories, and a Russian author to boot."

Hayleigh laughed, and Stephen told his grandmother he didn't get to read for fun as much as he used to, but he was glad she got the book she wanted.

"Well." She lifted her hands to look at them. "I wasn't expecting anyone. And I don't have the guest beds made up, but that won't take a minute—we can do it later." She went to the sink, where she ran the tap hard and scraped her fingers across a bar of soap.

Beneath the loud rush of water Hayleigh whispered, "I thought you said she was eighty."

"She is."

After she turned the water off and was wiping her hands on a dish towel, Stephen said, "We didn't come to stay, Gram. Just dropping by to say hi. We're on our way to the lake."

"Oh. Nice! Well, in that case, I don't imagine you want to stay very long." She reached for the kettle. "Anybody want tea?"

"We're allowed to check in at three o'clock," Hayleigh said.

"I'll have some tea, thanks." Stephen took a seat at the table, but Hayleigh asked to use the bathroom. He got up to show her where it was. When he came back to the kitchen, his grandmother put the mug down in front of him and said, "Are you telling me the semester's over already? You've been a college student for a whole year?"

"Yeah, we had exams last week." He looked down and blushed in advance of his next words. "I'm pretty sure I got a 4.0."

"Good for you! Though I can't say I'm surprised." She

touched his hand. "I don't think I'm telling you something you don't already know, but your mother was pretty worried when you first got there. That the school was too big or 'not a good fit'—that seems to be a phrase they use these days. That you weren't making friends. But obviously you've made *some* friends." Smiling, she nodded toward the closed bathroom door. "Do you two have classes together?"

"No, totally different. She's a marketing major."

"So did you meet at a party?"

"Nah. There was this physics competition, it was kind of a big deal with a lot of schools. I won a medal." The blush again.

"Impressive." His grandmother's expression showed pleasure. "And obviously she"— another nod in the direction of the hallway—"was impressed, too."

"I don't know." He shrugged. "She says I make her look good, but. You know. It's the other way around."

His grandmother took a quick breath in through her nostrils; it was not a sniff as much as the sound of someone reacting to a sharp and sudden pain. When it appeared to have passed, she said in a fierce whisper, "You don't need anyone else to make you look good." He smiled at her but covered his eyes with his hand for a moment, until the bathroom door opened and Hayleigh emerged.

Instead of joining them in the kitchen, she began examining the various framed items on the hallway wall. "So, who's this black guy in the baseball uniform?"

In unison, Stephen and his grandmother told her, "Jackie Robinson."

"I don't know who that is."

His grandmother raised her eyebrows, then nodded at Stephen to answer. "First black player in the major leagues. He integrated the game."

His grandmother stood from the table to join Hayleigh

in the hall. "I wrote him a fan letter when I was thirteen. I won't mention the year." She pointed. "See that postcard under the picture? That's what he wrote back."

"*Dear Ruth*," Hayleigh read aloud, "*Enjoyed reading your letter. Thanks for all those nice things you said about me. Sincerely.*" She stepped back for a longer view. "It's probably a form letter; you could write that to anyone."

Stephen's grandmother said quietly, "I prefer to think he wrote it to *me*. If you don't mind."

"Tea's getting cold," Stephen said from the table.

The women came back to sit with him. "Excuse me if I was a little short," his grandmother said to Hayleigh. "It's just that he's always been a hero of mine. My father used to take me to see him at Ebbets Field. When he first started playing, people would spit at him and call him all kinds of names. They made threats, too. But he just kept doing what was the right thing to do." She stared into her tea as if searching for the best words to say next. "He was an unusual man. A man of courage."

Hayleigh appeared to consider this before responding. "I guess you have a different definition than I do. I know a guy who jumps off cliffs in Mexico. Or my cousin who's a cop in D.C. *That's* courage."

Stephen's grandmother said, "Well, yes. But a different kind. What I'm talking about is someone taking a stand for something even when he knows what he'll suffer because of it." She shook her head. "I could never be that brave."

"Yes you could, Gram. You *were*." Stephen tapped a forefinger on the table as if to point out to her where she was wrong. "When you got your divorce. I know how hard that was for you; Mom told me. Kicking him out and then having to go get that job at the bus office. Most women would have just put up with it, Mom said. But you did the braver thing."

Hayleigh said, "*My* mother just put up with it."

"A lot of women were doing that, especially back then." Stephen's grandmother dismissed his compliment with a curl of her lips. "Leaving—I wouldn't call that courage. Thank you, but I wouldn't call it that. It was fortitude, maybe. Or survival." She smiled, perhaps at the younger version of herself, before looking serious again. "But what he did"—she gestured at the souvenir in the hallway—"that's something else. A moral courage, I guess you could call it."

"I wish my mother had done what you did," Hayleigh said. "I probably would have turned out to be a lot better person than the one I am right now."

"Oh, I don't believe in that." Stephen's grandmother raised and lowered her teabag in her empty mug. "You kids are grown-ups now. You can be any kind of person you choose." She shifted and put both hands down to press herself up from the table. "I'm getting some more hot water—Stephen, you?"

That was when it happened—during her transition from sit to stand. A small but sharp, unmistakable noise of gas emitted from her body, a shocking spurt of indignity in the otherwise quiet room.

The sound sent an immediate flush to the cheeks of both Stephen and his grandmother, and Hayleigh giggled. Stephen's grandmother mustered a faint smile. "I guess I'm not as much in control of things as I used to be." She seemed to have forgotten that she'd intended to get the kettle, and she stood at the table's edge smoothing the tablecloth under fingers she had not quite managed to scrub clean. "I'm sure you kids want to get going. It's almost two o'clock."

Stephen said, "No, we have time," but Hayleigh got up, and in a louder voice than his, she said, "That's a good idea, I want to get there before it rains," and so Stephen rose to join her. As they said good-bye at the door, his grandmother told them she was sorry she hadn't known they were coming, or she would have been a better hostess. "You were great," Stephen said, and she took his head between her hands for a moment while Hayleigh wasn't looking, then waved them on their way.

"That was wicked funny," Hayleigh said when they were on the road again. "She goes all philosophical on us about how we can decide what kind of people we want to be, and then she rips one." She laughed again, letting it dwindle slowly.

"Can you pull up the directions?" Stephen pointed at her phone, onto which she was furiously tapping a message that appeared to rekindle her amusement. "I don't think we're as close as I thought we were."

He joined her in the singing she wanted to do for the remainder of the trip. When finally they pulled onto the road leading to the resort, she whistled and said, "Whoa. Even on a day like this, this place is gorgeous." A bellhop led them to the harbor side of the building, unlocking the door to an enormous room with a galley kitchen and a view of the lake. After the bellhop had left with his tip, Hayleigh said, "This must have cost a fortune. When you said you wanted us to be together somewhere besides your crappy apartment or my crappy dorm room, I wasn't expecting *this*." She swept her arm across the picture window, through which two kayaks were visible. "Are they going out or coming in?"

"I can't tell," Stephen said. "I hope coming in, for their sake. It's supposed to be a bad storm."

She squinted in order to see the boats better. "They can't see us, can they?"

"No, I'm pretty sure not. Why?"

She shivered. "Because I can't stand being seen if I can't see the person back." She turned from the window to look again around the room. "Are your parents paying for all this?"

"No. I am." He touched his chest as if he worried she

might not realize who he meant. "I have that money from my internship. Why would you think I'd take money from my parents?"

She shrugged. "I don't know. Just, your mother packed you *brownies*." She motioned at the tinfoil package he'd carried in from the car and placed on the galley counter over the mini-fridge.

"She made those for both of us. I know, I wish she hadn't, either." He stepped forward to lift her hair from her shoulders, then kissed the back of her neck. "But making brownies isn't the same as paying for a romantic weekend with my girlfriend."

"Just a sec, okay?" She turned to lift his hand to her breast under her shirt, then pulled it out again. "I'll be right back."

While she was in the bathroom, he sat on the edge of the bed and looked out at the kayaks. Now it was possible to tell that they had moved closer to the shore than when Hayleigh had asked if the people in them could see her. Stephen stood up and pulled the drapes, then went over to the bathroom door when from inside Hayleigh called to him. "Sweetie, could you run out and get me some maxi pads?"

A pause before he said, "Where would be the best place to get them, do you think?"

"Oh, for God's sake." She opened the door smiling and with triumph in her eyes. "I was *kidding*. I haven't used a pad since I was twelve." She put a hand on his arm. "You'd really do that for me? Oh, that actually makes my heart hurt." She raised the hand to her chest.

They moved closer to the bed and flopped on it together. Hayleigh suggested they get under the covers, so they did. "Remember you said once we got here, I could call all the shots? This is the shot I call. Although I'm guessing it's the shot you'd want to be calling, too."

He murmured a sound of assent. "You were right," she said after a few minutes during which they shucked their clothes and began kissing. "This is much better than your apartment or my dorm room. This makes it something to remember."

But after another few minutes, Stephen threw the comforter aside and sat up. "What's the matter?" Hayleigh asked, reaching to touch his back. "You okay?"

He swung his legs over the side of the bed, then dug his hands into the skin on top of both thighs and pressed it away from him, toward the knees. Hayleigh raised herself on an elbow, one breast visible behind the fallen-away sheet. "Stop it. You're hurting yourself."

He stopped, though still kept his back to her. "You laughed at my grandmother."

"What?" She scooted closer to his side of the bed, and he repeated what he'd said.

"You're kidding, right? You mean when she farted? So what, it was funny. I mean, it's funny when anyone farts, but an old lady, even more."

"I didn't think it was funny." He turned halfway toward her, as if to make sure she'd hear.

"Stop being such a snowflake. Anyway, she didn't notice."

"Of course she noticed. How could she not notice? You were sitting right in front of her."

Hayleigh peered at him with the expression of someone trying to identify an almost familiar species of creature she'd come upon by surprise. Then her face changed—she smiled—and she gave his shoulder a friendly, playful slap. "Come on. Let's do something more fun than talking about your grandmother's poot."

"I can't." He said it at the lowest possible volume above a whisper. From the look on his face, an observer might have concluded that he was trying to contain what followed, but knew he would fail. "I don't want to be with someone who would do a thing like that."

She recoiled as if struck. "*Asshole*." But the word sounded weak coming out of her. It was less spit than gasped.

"I'm sorry," Stephen said.

"You know what? You actually *do* look sorry. And that only makes it worse." She leapt up from the bed, yanking the sheet to wrap it clumsily around her, and hop-tripped toward the bathroom. Once inside, she slammed the door and turned the sink faucet on at full blast.

Stephen stared down at the carpet beneath his feet. When she came out of the bathroom, she said, "I took a total chance on you, you know. Do you get that? Do you think I didn't have *major* second thoughts about hooking up with a guy like you?"

"I do get that," Stephen said. Again it was barely a murmur.

"I should have known." She seemed to be speaking more to herself than to him. "Don't look at me," she said, so he kept his eyes on the floor. She hurried her clothes on and rummaged loudly until she found her phone.

"What are you doing?"

"Calling a ride."

"Don't be silly." He stood to face her, but she crossed her fingers and held them up to ward him off. "I'll drive you back."

"No, you know what's *silly*? You thinking I would ever want to spend all that time with you in a car again. What a complete and total *waste*." She reached for the doorknob, then turned to deliver her final inspired line. Before she could do so, he closed his eyes. "And don't think for a minute that I'm not going to tell people about this. You're the one who comes off bad in this story, not me."

After she was gone, he stood looking at the door for a few moments before moving to the kitchen area and opening the package of brownies. He ate three within a minute, barely taking time to swallow, and reached for a fourth. But instead of biting into it, he paused, as if an invisible hand had tapped his own in admonition, then replaced the brownie in the tinfoil before putting the remainder of the batch in the mini-fridge. The half-finished one, which Hayleigh had started eating in the car and then rejected, he dropped into the trash can beneath the mini-peninsula.

Crossing the room to the windows, he opened the drapes to find that the clouds had grown thicker since he'd closed them. He stepped out to the balcony overlooking the harbor, putting both hands on the rail. The kayaks were still approaching, close to where they would eventually land. A woman paddled one and a man the other, and their voices carried indistinctly across the sound.

When they were twenty yards from shore and almost near enough to see him, Stephen stood and took a few steps toward the door leading back to the room. "You bastard! I *hate* you," the woman said, her voice suddenly as clear as if she stood beside him. She had an accent like the actress on the series Stephen's mother loved, about a female prime minister of Denmark. Stephen swiveled quickly, but the woman was laughing. It was a fake blow she delivered to her companion as they stepped out to the shore. "Remind me to bring some other jackass next time," she told him, before they kissed with a quick smack and pulled the kayaks onto the sand.

The boats secured, they ascended the beach. They were huge people, both of them: tall and broad in a way that was not overweight, but only strong; together they might have been able to turn back the waves moving shoreward, at least for a moment or two. The woman caught sight of Stephen on the balcony, and gesturing at the sky, she called, "Just in time!" in a manner she might use with someone she recognized. As the first drops fell, he lifted a hand back. The woman put her arm around the man's waist as they headed away from Stephen, and the man put his arm around hers. They leaned into each other. Watching, Stephen draped his own arm across his own waist and peered after the receding figures, as if doing his best to keep them in sight even after they'd disappeared.

DIVERTIMENTO

Half past noon on a weekday, the middle of summer. Sunny and hot. The flags outside the municipal buildings sway not in the least, which is a way of saying that the air is as still as it can possibly be—not even the premonition of a breeze, even for those who have premonitions.

In the historic part of the city, two women are having lunch on one of the benches surrounding a public playground. Now when I say "bench," you may be picturing a strictly utilitarian apparatus, a mere slab of a seat. But in fact, these benches are nearly like sofas. They've been designed with more than mere utility in mind: they are for parents and teachers who need a place to sit while they supervise children on seesaws and monkey bars; retirees who come here to read, or to remind themselves of the routines they used to inhabit; and working people like Eve and Petra who meet once in a while on their lunch break, who prefer to do so outdoors when the weather is good, and whose experience of their hour together is enhanced many times over by the fact that they can share the wide, curved, cushiony surface made of a soft yet indestructible polymer and, when they tire of sitting upright, lean against a backrest of the same material, placed at just the right distance and angle in relation to the seat. (At the unveiling, dozens of toss pillows provided color and decoration, but those have of course long since disappeared.) And yes, since you may be wondering, there are armrests, too.

When the benches first appeared, replacing the old, hard, backless ones, the two women remarked almost every time they met about how amazing it was: such a treat, so unexpected. But that was a number of years ago. It's been ages since they've mentioned it now.

The women are not young anymore by most standards—that's important to know. They're both approaching the middle of middle age.

Petra has brought her usual: a sandwich, chips, and an apple packed from home. Eve always buys her lunch from one of the many vendors lining the cobblestone path leading to the playground, which lies almost exactly halfway between the buildings in which the women work. Petra has a more important and higher-paying job than Eve, although Eve likes her job more than Petra likes hers.

Today Eve has picked up souvlaki, which she unwraps slowly after she and Petra greet each other and sit down. It is only with Petra that she chooses what to her are exotic foods, even though the exoticism of Petra herself (mostly owing to the foreign sound of her name) wore off long ago. Petra has no way of knowing it, but Eve is considering putting an end to these lunches, occasional though they are. The past few times—well, more than that, really—Petra's mood has been dark, and her energy low, and it really does Eve no good at all to be around her. It was one thing at the beginning, when she was kind of fascinated by what she perceived, falsely as it turned out, to be Petra's worldliness. But now it's just, frankly, a drag.

Eve feels guilty for thinking this way, because if she were a true friend, wouldn't she ask Petra if something was wrong? And if she could help?

But it doesn't actually feel like true friendship. They met at the fortieth birthday dinner of a mutual friend, and discovered they worked near each other. These lunches started out pleasant enough, and it's convenient, but nothing more. If Eve weren't already in the city because of her job, and taking a break at midday anyway, she wouldn't be meeting Petra for lunch or anything else.

A red rubber ball rolls near their feet, and one of the children from the playground calls to ask if they will send it back over the fence. Petra either hasn't heard the request or is pretending not to have heard it, so Eve puts down her souvlaki, picks up the ball, and drop-kicks it back to where the children are waiting. A few of the kids snicker, old enough to be amused by the sight of a woman who could be their grandmother kicking a ball with the toe of her pointy, professional shoe.

But they would also have to admit to feeling impressed that she kicked it so well. Without hesitation, firmly, and confident in her aim. In fact, one of the boys will remember this image for most of his life, usually when he is called upon for courage—to do something he is afraid of and thinks he cannot do.

When Eve sits back down to resume eating her sandwich, Petra tells her, "I'm no good at sports," as if this has do to with anything.

And something in what she sees in her "friend" then—the slump of Petra's shoulders, the frown in her brow—causes Eve to snap, as it were, and she smashes the slim but well-built wall, the one made of politeness, that has always existed between them. "What is the matter with you? I haven't seen you smile in months. I'm telling you, it's too much . . . lately when I go back to work after seeing you, I have a bad afternoon, or I just about fall asleep at my desk."

None of this seems to surprise Petra, which surprises Eve. Does this mean she could or should have said something sooner? Petra looks not surprised, but even sadder than she did before. "I tried to throw the ball back once," she explains, "and it hit the top of the fence and punctured on one of those metal spikes. The kids laughed. Some of them even booed."

"So what? They're children."

Petra shakes her head. "You don't understand. When you're sensitive, everything cuts the same, whether it's big or little."

Eve keeps herself from speaking the phrase that occurs to her, which is *pity party*.

Petra goes on to say, "I read a lot of books," as if this has to do with anything. "I didn't use to, but now I do. Ever since Gil and I . . ." But she has never in Eve's experience finished a sentence that includes her ex-husband's name.

". . . ?" Now Eve is the one who frowns, fumbling for a response. "Well, that's good, isn't it? It's great that you read books. Too many people don't." *I* don't, she doesn't add, because it dismays her that this has become the case.

"But *is* it great?" Petra shades her eyes against the sun. "I'm not so sure. I've been reading things lately, the Russians, that make me think I should be looking for a different kind of book. Books that don't ask questions. Books that don't make me think. Maybe I would be happier."

". . . ?" Again, Eve can think of nothing to offer by way of following up.

"They talk a lot about the meaning of life. Whether life *has* any meaning. Take the one I'm reading now." Petra reaches into her bag to pull out a paperback. "Basically, the author says that everything we do, every action we take, is only aimed at distracting us from the fact that it all ends in death."

"A sort of 'Life sucks and then you die' kind of thing?" As soon as it leaves her mouth, Eve regrets her sarcasm, but luckily, Petra seems not to notice or to mind.

"Some of them seem to think that if life *does* have meaning," she concedes, "that meaning is love. The connections we make with other people, and with ourselves. There's this one story about a woman who talks to her sugar bowl. It just sits there on her table, and she becomes friends with it. I like that one a lot."

"Well, there you go! What's wrong with that?" Eve had not expected to hear so much relief in her own voice.

"That's easy for you to say—you *have* love."

Oh, dear. Is Petra asking Eve to say she loves her? She can't do it—it isn't true.

But before she can figure out how to respond, Petra has reached over to grab her by the arm, almost as if she hasn't even realized it. Aside from the hugs they exchange when they meet and part each time—which, in the way of such things, are not really hugs—they have never touched each other. What is this?!

"Are you saying it hasn't happened to you yet? Because I don't believe it. At our age it happens more often than not—the lying awake at night, wondering what you've done with your life, where all that time's gone, and how much you have left. And on top of that, wondering, *What is the point?*"

Eve shakes off Petra's hand with more resentment and vigor than she would have liked to reveal. "What a cliché! And if you don't mind, I came here to have a nice lunch, not talk about dying!" She looks up at the clock on the bank tower, wishing she were back in her office instead of sitting on this bench next to Petra. Then she tells herself, *Stop*—that isn't being mindful. It isn't being *here*. She's been advised that trying to be mindful, and here, will improve her experience of life. "Who says you have to believe what's in that book?" She nods at the paperback.

"I'm not sure what you're getting at," Petra says. She puts the other half of her sandwich away, as if the turn of their conversation has spoiled her appetite.

"I'm just saying that you could choose to have a different opinion. You could decide for yourself that life has any meaning you want." Eve is not entirely sure where she's going with this, but she likes the sound of it—she likes hearing something remotely intellectual, maybe even remotely profound, in her own voice. She licks the last of the yogurt sauce, which has a fancier name she always forgets, from her fingers. As usual, she neglected to pick up any napkins from the vendor's stand, and this makes her irritated at herself.

Petra feels her lips give off a brief but violent quiver, and wonders if Eve notices. Probably not, she decides. After all, they are sitting less across from each other than side by side, and she's never been particularly impressed by Eve's powers of perception.

But Eve is more on the ball than Petra gives her credit for. "You think those kids are worried about any of that?" She gestures widely toward the playground, upon which the sun has chosen to direct its strongest rays. "Whether life has any meaning? They couldn't care less."

Petra follows the track of Eve's hand, then shakes her head. "No. But that's exactly my point. They don't know about death yet."

"Well, neither do you. Not really. We can only know it in the abstract."

"What?!" Can Eve really be saying this? Petra hardly believes what she's hearing. "I watched both of my parents die. I took care of both of them at the end . . . I know death as well as anyone alive can know it!"

"And that's exactly *my* point." It feels good to Eve, being able to say this. Somehow, she realizes, she's always assumed that Petra's depression makes her the smarter of the two of them. Not so—right? At least she is determined to divest herself of that idea. A person can be happy and smart at the same time. Though she knows people who would disagree with her, she refuses to believe that the two can't coexist.

She must have murmured something without realizing, because Petra says, "What?"

Eve shakes her head. "I'm thinking of something I want to say to you, but I don't know whether it'll make you feel better or worse. It usually makes *me* feel better, but I think we might be different in that."

"What is it?" If Petra's trying to conceal the fact that she's intrigued—hopeful, even—it isn't working.

"It's from a sign on a Buddhist temple in Thailand."

"Wait—you've been to Thailand?"

How greatly Eve wishes to respond that yes, she has! How greatly she wishes for a single exotic experience of her own. Too late, she'd realized that of course Petra would ask. And how much Eve also wishes to avoid confessing the truth, which is that she saw the temple inscription only on social media.

But she prides herself more than anything on being a person who—despite feeling tempted, she's working on that—doesn't allow herself to put on airs that she hasn't earned. "No, it's just a post I saw, a photo, by someone I know who *did* go. Anyway, the sign over the door says: *Remember, one hundred years from now, all new people.*"

She draws out the last three words because they are, of course, the important ones. They are, after all, the point. Watching Petra's eyes, she can tell that it takes a moment for the meaning to sink in—as, Eve recalls, it did with her. Then she sees the click of Petra comprehending, before the dam finally gives way. "Why did you have to tell me that? Isn't that another way of saying that everything's irrelevant—whatever any of us do—because it will all be forgotten and we're all going to be replaced anyway? Doesn't it reinforce what those Russians are writing about, that none of it means anything?"

Though the same has occurred to Eve herself, she's chosen to reject this interpretation. "No. What I'm saying, what *it's* saying, is that whatever we're worried or sad about, in the long run it's not a big deal. Doesn't that take some of the pressure off? Doesn't that make you feel . . . I don't know, lighter?"

But Petra's crying. For God's sake! Eve's not going to sit here and listen to that.

"I think you need to dwell in possibility," she continues, before Petra can deliver another morose rebuff. The phrase—*dwell in possibility*—popped into Eve's head as she cast around for a path out of this pity party, though she could not name the quote's source. Probably it is etched on one of the decorative stones a hippie friend of hers at work keeps in a shallow dish on her desk, for inspiration. *Believe. This too shall pass. The best is yet to come.*

"All these sayings. They're just so much hot air." Petra waves dismissively. At least she isn't crying anymore. She places the bag with her remaining half sandwich into her purse, as if preparing to take off. Eve would be fine—*more* than fine—with her leaving, but instead Petra says, "Tell me what you mean by 'possibility,'" sounding almost as if she might be doing Eve a favor by asking.

Once, at work, Eve was directed at the last minute to lead a meeting on a subject she knew nothing about. She feels that way now, forced to occupy the head of a table at which people sit waiting for her to educate them.

"Well, just look around you, it's everywhere," she says vaguely. The first thing *she* sees, looking around, is the playground. "One of those kids might grow up to do something remarkable someday. *More* than one of them might. Invent something. Cure cancer."

"Oh, please. Why not just say, 'They're the hope of the future'? I mean really, talk about a cliché."

"Well, then, *you* might do something remarkable. You might feel something you never expected to feel." *Who's the hippie now?* she says then, but only inside her own head.

Petra has truly hoped for an answer she could hang her

hat on. Instead what she gets is this mindless pablum about *possibility* . . . what a crock. "If we don't die of cancer, we'll just die of something else. And all those kids might just as easily end up homeless or on drugs. Or depressed, like me. At best they'll be automatons, living inside their phones like all the rest of them."

Why had she thought today might be different? She woke up hoping that something might come along to change her heart. But clearly, it isn't going to be lunch with Eve that does it.

By now, though, Eve has grown invested in convincing Petra. Or is it in convincing herself? And of what, again? Oh, right—the idea that life is worth living. That it all has meaning, even if we can't figure out what it is. That there's some purpose to being here.

Are those all the same, or three separate things?

"You're impossible!" she cries out. "Okay, if you need something less abstract, then take this bench."

"Mmmm?"

"This bench. How comfy it is. Remember how bad those old benches used to be? We almost stopped coming, we were going to meet somewhere else. But we couldn't decide where, so we came to the park one last time, and here was this new bench just waiting for us. You can see how much thought and care went into it. First, in the design. Then a prototype, which I'm sure the company tested on regular people like us. Asked them questions. Improved and adjusted things, according to the feedback they heard. Then produced them to spec, and installed them in this park, all so we could have a more comfortable place to sit while we eat our lunch and argue about whether anything in this world is worth doing, whether it has any meaning at all."

Saying this takes Eve's breath away. At work and at home, she hardly ever utters more than one sentence at a time.

"Oh, please. You're not going to say 'It's the little things,' are you?"

"No," Eve says, although she had been.

"And you act as if they did it out of concern for us." Petra clutches her purse to her side even though she is still seated. "Purely for our comfort. When, in fact, they did it for money."

"So? Why shouldn't they get paid for a job well done—for something that's useful to somebody else, or to the world? Would you do *your* job if you weren't getting paid? Of course not." Eve makes a more obnoxious sound than she intended, emphasizing this conclusion. To temper it, she modulates her tone and adds, "My point is, there's always the possibility that something—a situation, a person, a mood—will change for the better."

"Or for the worse," Petra says.

"Well, of course, but the odds are fifty-fifty, aren't they? Why not anticipate they'll land on the 'better' side?" When Petra doesn't answer, Eve lets momentum propel her forward. "*Do* you remember how it used to feel, sitting here? My butt would get numb. Now, it's practically like sitting on a couch in my own living room. It's made a difference in my life, this bench, and in yours, too, whether you admit it or not."

Petra admits, "Yes, it has made a difference." Her voice is little more than a murmur, but it's loud enough to be heard.

"This moment *right now* is better for us than it would be, if not for this bench." She's almost got it, Eve thinks. What she feels creeping up to her comprehension, what she wants to express. The answer to Petra's question: *Tell me what you mean by "possibility."*

But now, interrupting, comes the same red rubber ball from the playground, rolling again at their feet. The kids clamor at the fence, repeating the call for the women to send it back.

"Your turn this time," Eve says, annoyed that the ball has bounced the insight—the revelation?—straight out of her head.

"But they'll laugh at me."

"If you don't try, how will you find out? Maybe this time they won't."

Petra smiles the smile of someone who knows better, picks up the ball, takes a few steps toward the playground, and tosses it as high as she can. To her surprise, it lands precisely in front of the child who'd kicked it by accident out of bounds, a first-grader who bullies kids his own age but—because he has been punished for doing otherwise—will, for another year or two beyond now, treat adults with the respect he's been told they deserve. "Thanks, lady!" he shouts, picking it up before running back to his friends.

"That means nothing," Petra tells Eve, returning to the bench. "That hardly proves your point."

Eve's smile is also the smile of one who knows better. But they can't both be right—or can they? By mutual agreement, and because the clock on the bank tower shows them it's time, they dispose of their trash, "hug" good-bye, and head in opposite directions toward their respective desks. Petra looks down at her feet, afraid as always of tripping over a cobblestone. Eve puts in her earbuds so she can listen to her favorite divertimento on the way back. The sun seems higher than it did when she arrived in the park at noon, though she knows this cannot be. She lifts her eyes and squints against it, panicked in momentary blindness before comes the relief of again being able to see.

The children on the playground laugh as she passes, but she decides not to contemplate why.

GHOST STORY

It was the hottest July on record, and years later, Miranda would remember about that summer neither of the two funerals but the way her hair clung to the back of her neck as she and her brother set up their lemonade stand. Their mother had taken them to the beverage distribution center to buy cheap cans of soda, which they offered along with pitchers of yellow and pink lemonade they had made themselves by adding water from the kitchen faucet to packets of crystals. The soda they kept in a cooler, where Miranda propped her feet as they waited for people to come by. Her brother, Charlie, who passed the time stomping on ants, had made a sign on the plastic easel they'd used when they were little to draw pictures their mother would then hang on the fridge. *Mercer Street Cafe*, he wrote at the top of the long paper secured to the board by a giant blue clip. *Cans or cups of refreshment = 25 ¢.*

Miranda's friend Bailey Rose had come over to help with the stand, and she was doing hula hoops by Charlie's sign— "to attract customers," she said. Miranda thought Bailey was showing off, and she wanted to use the hula hoop herself, but Bailey was a guest, and she knew what her mother would say. She waited for Bailey to tire out. In the meantime, Charlie kept telling them to come over and look at the ants' guts. The girls refused. Cars stopped and people they knew from the neighborhood got out to buy things to drink. Miranda used her old Fisher Price cash register to collect money and return change. Most of the people were from Mercer Street, on their way home after work, but they came from other blocks, too.

"You're very enterprising, girls," Mr. Holworthy said to them, after draining his cup and giving them a dollar, which he let them keep. They didn't know what he meant by that, but they said thank you anyway. When he drove off, they laughed. Maggie Holworthy was in their class, and she wore the wrong kind of shoes. Some of the boys called her "Maggot," and Miranda didn't know what this meant, either, but the idea that they might ever say something like that about *her*, and then laugh about it, was too much to think about.

They were about to close up the stand—it was almost time for dinner—when a fancy-looking red convertible approached and slowed down in front of the house. Miranda squinted, but she couldn't tell who was inside. She knew it was a Miata because her brother wanted one, bad, even though he wouldn't be able to get a license for another six years. She had a premonition that the person inside the car had not stopped for lemonade.

The door opened and her Aunt Valerie got out of the driver's seat, her hair going every which way from being blown around in the wind. Miranda almost didn't know who it was for a moment, because Valerie's hair had gotten a lot longer, and it was a different color, too. "Hi, Boo!" Valerie called to Miranda as she came toward the lemonade stand. "Hey, bud," she said to Charlie.

"Aunt Val," Charlie said, and took the first hug, to get it over with. Miranda knew that as much as he loved their aunt, he hated hugs more. "Cool car," he said, daring to touch it, as Valerie hugged Miranda and then reached to include Bailey in it, too. Bailey smiled shyly and let the hula hoop fall to the ground.

"I'll give you a ride later," Valerie told Charlie. "Maybe I'll even let you take a turn at the wheel." She winked at him, and Miranda could tell that even though he knew it wasn't going to happen, her brother got excited about just the idea.

"What are you doing here?" Miranda asked, before she recognized that her mother would have labeled the question rude. But her aunt didn't appear to take offense.

"I decided to surprise you all." Valerie went back to the car and pulled out a red suitcase. "Remember at Christmastime, I had to pull over on the Thruway and wait out that freak snowstorm? But today somebody up there must like me—I made it in six hours flat."

"Is that *Val?*" Miranda's mother stepped out of the house, and when she recognized her sister, she came running out to the curb in her bare feet, causing Miranda to worry that she was stepping on the dead ants. "What are you doing here? Why didn't you call?" They hugged hard, until Miranda wondered if they were hurting each other.

"I just got in the car and took off. I had to see you." Valerie lifted her sunglasses to search her sister's face. "It's okay, isn't it?"

"Of course it is. It's just that I wouldn't have thought— well, never mind. This is a real treat, isn't it, kids? Come inside—you must be exhausted." Miranda's mother went to pick up Valerie's suitcase, but her sister waved her off and insisted on lugging it herself toward the front porch.

The children abandoned the lemonade stand. Ordinarily, their mother would not have let them do this—she would have made them clean everything up—but now she was distracted by Valerie's visit, so all they did was bring the money inside. They'd made seven dollars and seventy-five cents. Charlie gave the girls two-fifty each and kept the extra quarter for himself, because he was the oldest. Miranda knew this wasn't fair, but she also knew her mother would tell them to work it out if they bothered her about it, so she just took the money and put it into her *Kim Possible* bank.

She was saving up for a trip to Disney World. She didn't know when it would happen, but she was going to go. She had to. She had never even been on a plane before, and here Bailey Rose went to Florida every winter and came back with souvenirs like an Ariel doll and a music box that played "It's a Small World." The hotel she stayed in had a waterslide that started three levels up and spun you in a long spiral before shooting you into the pool. She sent Miranda a postcard every year, and when she received it, Miranda taped it next to her bed and felt jealous of Bailey until she fell asleep.

Bailey went home, and Miranda and Charlie turned on the TV while their mother and Valerie talked in the kitchen. "I forgot, you're not supposed to drink with the—" Miranda heard her mother say, but Valerie cut her off. "Oh, don't worry about it. It doesn't affect me."

"I'd hate to make you sick, though."

"You won't. I drink wine with dinner every night."

"But a gin and tonic, on top of—"

"I said don't *worry*, Cher. I'll be fine." Then there was the sound of ice clinking, and her mother's sigh.

Miranda stopped listening, because her father was home. "Whose car?" he asked Charlie and Miranda in a low voice as he stepped through the door.

"Aunt Val's here," Miranda said. "A surprise."

"Valerie? She drove herself here?" He lifted a hand, showing a wet circle under his armpit, and ran his fingers through the back of his sweaty hair.

Miranda asked, "Why not?" Her brother barely even noticed that their father had come in. Charlie never wanted to know anything about anybody. He was happy just to watch TV or practice his hacky sack, which he wasn't supposed to play with in the house. He was playing hacky sack now, while watching *Buffy the Vampire Slayer*.

"Why?" Miranda said again when her father didn't answer her. "Why wouldn't she drive herself here? That's what she always does."

"Oh, nothing. Nothing, honey." Her father tossed his work clipboard onto the stairs as he did every night—to Miranda it always seemed as if he hoped it would explode or something, that's how hard he got rid of it—and went toward the kitchen. "Look who's here!" Miranda heard him say, followed by the sound of Valerie clapping him on the back as they embraced. Valerie asked, "What do you think?" and her father answered, "I like it. Do they make that with real hair, or what?" and Valerie said, "It's synthetic, but you can't tell, can you, Jim?" Miranda's father mumbled something in reply and then she couldn't tell what the grown-ups were talking about anymore. She muted the TV, but the voices in the kitchen were still too hard to make out, and Charlie made her turn it back up. Then their mother called them to dinner.

After they'd all sat down, Miranda's father asked, "Written any new stories lately?" Even Miranda recognized it as the question he always started out with when her aunt visited.

Usually, Valerie described what she was working on. But this time she made a face and said, "No, I haven't, Jim. What would I write about?"

Miranda's father sputtered. "I don't know, I just thought maybe—" He stopped himself, and Miranda focused on her meatloaf because something in the adults' voices made her heart speed up.

"Well, don't think. It's not your style." A moment later, after hearing her sister gasp, Valerie said, "Jim, I apologize. Please—forgive me. I'm sorry. *I'm* the one who's not thinking very well anymore." She lifted her fork, but held it over the plate without picking up any food. "It's just that I always used to think my next story would be *the one*—the one I spent my life building up to, the one that said everything I have inside me to say. I could almost see it in front of me, I could almost read the words . . . but now it's all vanished. I'm back to a blank page."

Miranda's father didn't seem to know how to respond to this; he sold cell phone plans for a living.

"Don't worry," Valerie said. "I've accepted that I'm never going to be Anya Chaykovskaya."

"Who?" Miranda's parents asked the question at the same time. From Valerie's tone, everyone at the table could tell she had not accepted this at all. Miranda's mother said, "I loved your last one, it made me cry," and even Miranda could tell that Valerie didn't believe her.

Valerie stayed for three days, and on each of them they went shopping, because she said she wanted to buy something special for everyone. "You shouldn't spend your money," Miranda's mother said, but Valerie insisted.

"What else am I going to do with my 'retirement account'?" she said, putting finger quotes around the words and giving a pretend laugh. "Retire?" Miranda's mother made a mouth movement and looked away. Charlie asked for a new Trek bike, so the next day—exactly at noon, because it was the hottest time and they knew the store would be air-conditioned—they got that. After putting off saying what she really wanted, Miranda's mother broke down and said she'd love a pair of those designer sandals with the silver butterflies, so in the middle of the second day, they drove into the city to find her some, along with a matching purse for good measure. At the hardware store, on the advice of her sister, Valerie bought a grill that Miranda's father had looked at, but hadn't bought himself because of how much it cost.

When it came to Miranda's turn, she hesitated to say what she had thought of the moment her aunt announced her plan to buy them all presents. But Valerie made her tell, so Miranda confessed, "A puppy?" and Valerie exclaimed, "Perfect!"

"Oh, no," Miranda's mother said. "You know what Jim would say about that. It's too much work, and when we go away, what would we do with it?"

Valerie exclaimed, "You just get someone to come in and walk it!" Miranda loved the way her aunt's bracelets jangled when she was excited; at least this was one thing that hadn't changed. "I'll find you a dog-sitter, as part of the gift."

"Val—"

"Please, Cherry. Let me do this."

"But Jim—"

"He'll say yes, and you know it."

Miranda only realized she'd been holding her breath, listening to her aunt and her mother argue, when she had to let it out in a big whoosh. When her mother said, "Well, let me ask," she felt a tingle at the top of her head, and a little fear, at the thought that she might actually be allowed to get a dog.

By the next morning Miranda's father had agreed, as Valerie had said he would, so at the stroke of noon Miranda and her mother and Valerie and Charlie headed to Pet Village. Miranda kept saying, "I can't believe I'm getting a puppy."

"What are you going to name it, Boo?" her aunt asked.

"I don't know yet."

"How about 'Val'?" Her aunt was turning in the front seat to smile, and for the first time Miranda allowed herself to identify the shadow in Valerie's eyes.

"That's *you*." Miranda felt the way she always did in school when she was supposed to understand what the teacher was talking about but didn't.

"It probably comes already named," Miranda's mother said, looking down at the ground as they walked toward the store.

Miranda went straight to a cocker spaniel, named Daniel, who lay quietly in a corner of his cage; she would not even look at any other dogs once the Pet Village employee let Daniel out. Valerie purchased the dog, and a bunch of other things the employee said Miranda would need, and they brought Daniel home. Miranda did not want to go to the pool for the rest of the day, as they had done on the other two afternoons of Valerie's visit. She said it was because she wanted to stay home with the dog, and in part this was true; but the real reason was that the day before, she had seen her aunt's hair slip sideways in the water, revealing stubble underneath, and the sight made everything go wavy in front of her eyes.

Aunt Val said she'd stay home with Miranda and Daniel. They could all take naps, she said. Daniel seemed happy with the plan, and Miranda tried, but she wasn't sleepy. On the other side of the thin bedroom wall, she could hear Valerie turning pages. Timidly she knocked, and when Valerie told her to come in, Miranda found her on the pull-out couch with an old, falling-apart book propped up against her knees. "What are you reading?" she asked.

"A poem."

"Do you like it?"

Valerie shrugged. "It's okay. Kind of dated. Do you want to hear it?"

Miranda nodded and sat on the edge of the bed. Valerie began reading with an odd slowness, as if she had to think about the pronunciation of each individual word. "*How many loved your moments of glad grace/And loved your beauty with love false or true?*" She paused to rub hard at a penciled-on eyebrow. "*But one man loved the pilgrim soul in you/and loved the sorrows of your changing face.*" Abruptly she shut the book and tossed it across the room. Some of the loose pages scattered on the floor.

"What's a pilgrim soul?" Miranda asked.

"I have no idea." Naptime was over, Valerie added. She just needed a minute or two, and then they could go out to the backyard and kick the soccer ball around if Miranda wanted.

That night Miranda asked if she could invite Bailey Rose over for dinner, because Bailey didn't have a dog, but wanted one, and Miranda knew she would be jealous. After a picnic of hamburgers on the patio, they made s'mores on the new grill while Daniel lay under the table, breathing in funny-sounding huffs because of the heat.

Valerie bent over to peer at the dog. "Hmm," she said, but when somebody asked, "What?" she just shook her head. Then she asked Charlie if he knew any ghost stories. He started to tell one he'd learned on a field-trip tour of an estate some rich guy had built at the turn of the twentieth century to look like a medieval castle. The tour guide told Charlie's class that the place was haunted by the spirit of a young woman whose family had owned the farm the rich guy had bought for a song and then razed to make way for his fancy new home. "In real life she tried to go after the guy in court, but they couldn't afford a lawyer," Charlie said. "So she had to come back as a ghost after she died, because she had unfinished business."

"Well, *that* I understand," Valerie said.

"When she came back as a ghost," Charlie went on, getting the smile on his face that meant he was about to do something he might get in trouble for, "she brought a dog with her for protection. Only she didn't love it enough, so it ran away. She never saw him again."

"Careful," Miranda's father warned, wiping chocolate off his chin.

Miranda suspected that this wasn't part of the real story. "Was the dog a ghost, too?" she asked, hoping to stump him.

"Of course he was. *Duh.*"

"Charles," her father said. "That's enough." Even though Miranda could tell her brother was making it up as he went along, she felt little prickles on the backs of her hands.

"That is one lame story," said Bailey Rose.

Charlie gave her a look that suggested he might have bopped her if the grown-ups hadn't been around. "So did she fix it?" Valerie asked, leaning forward. "The unfinished business?"

Charlie shrugged and yawned at the same time. "I don't remember."

Valerie started to say something further, but when she saw the expression on Miranda's mother's face, she backed down and murmured, "Okay."

They never heard the end. Aunt Val drove off the next day, and Miranda held Daniel on his leash as they waved good-bye from the front door. That afternoon, Daniel lay down on his side under the table and didn't want any water or food. When Valerie called to say she'd made it home all right, Miranda's mother told her, "The dog isn't doing so well. I don't know. Maybe it's heatstroke or something. If he's still the same tomorrow, I'll take him to a vet."

Miranda sat beside Daniel on the kitchen floor and rubbed his head. When she came back to see him after dinner, he was dead.

She didn't stop crying until long after her father had wrapped Daniel in a towel and set him on the back stoop. "We'll have a funeral tomorrow," he told Miranda. "We'll bury him in the yard, and you can make a gravestone for him."

"With what," she said, still sobbing, but the idea of making a gravestone intrigued her a little.

In the morning she felt stuffy from all the crying she had done. She came downstairs and heard her mother on the phone. "I don't know, Val. What do you think? She cried. Of course she cried." Her mother listened a moment and added, "She cried for a long time. Is that what you wanted to hear?"

While her mother was talking, Miranda opened the back door to look outside. Daniel was still lying there, a lump under the towel. She heard a horn beep, and raised her head to see Maggie Holworthy waving from her father's car on the way to geology camp. "Maggot," Miranda whispered as she waved back, trying the word out on her tongue. Too late, she realized she'd made a mistake. Instead of a dog, she should have asked for a trip to Disney World. Then it would all still be ahead of her—the plane ride, and the fun.

That summer of the funerals stayed with her until it sank quietly into her mind and was heaped over by an accumulation of thousands of impressions, for nearly fifteen years. One day she was sitting in her car outside the TJ Maxx where she worked, trying to summon what it always took for her to go into that job, putting it off minute by minute by telling herself she'd move the next time her phone showed a new time, then the next new time, when, without warning, plain and clear in its true colors as if she looked through a screen at the scene that had not changed since the day it happened, the sight of the dead dog under the kitchen table leapt from its burial place to the center of her mind's eye. In the next moment it was replaced by the image of her aunt standing in blue water, grabbing suddenly at her hair—not her *hair*, stupid, a wig!—and yanking it to cover the shorn spots before paddling over to Miranda and asking if she wanted to be lifted high and then tossed in the shallow end.

It was a very hot day and the AC in her car didn't work, so she sat in the parking lot with her windows open and felt her own hair, thick and strong and fast-growing, sticking with sweat to the back of her neck. Inside the store she would lift it up and secure it with a clip per her supervisor's orders, but until then she let it stay spread against her skin like something not attached to her but separate, a comforting pressure or presence, anchoring her to herself. She felt it behind her neck as she had on the day she and her brother and Bailey Rose ran the lemonade stand: the day she had remembered vaguely until now as the time Aunt Val arrived out of nowhere and offered them all gifts. Instantly upon this thought, the dreadful visions faded, and she saw herself on the front lawn of the house she had almost forgotten, standing again in the blazing sunshine, again eight years old, smiling with her brother as they watched their favorite person drive up to surprise them in her magnificent red car.

A FLYING BIRD

The cake, on the floor of the front passenger seat, caught her eye as she walked by the car.

Wait! What was it doing on the floor? Why not the seat itself? There was plenty of room there; the only thing on it, besides a crumpled tissue, was a library book. Turned face-down, so the title couldn't be seen.

Cate could think of only two reasons for this, or maybe three: the borrower didn't want the book to be stolen; the borrower didn't feel like advertising her reading tastes to just anyone who might pass by; the borrower had tossed the book onto the seat and it landed that way.

She knew that the driver of this car must be a woman (lipstick stain on the tissue) and guessed reason number two for the turned-over book. Even more of an effort had been made to conceal the cake, tucked as it was on the floor mat halfway under the passenger seat.

Please be locked, she begged with the voice in her mind, crossing to the driver's side so that an observer would assume she was opening the door to her own car. But it wasn't.

Congratulations, honey! the cake said across the top in red frosted letters. *We love you*. This was almost enough to make Cate retreat and close the door, but she also knew she would not do so. As she took the cake out, she was tempted, so tempted, to turn over the library book to see its title— she could make out that the author's name was a long one ending in a vowel, possibly Russian, and on the back cover the appealing image of a sugar bowl set on a kitchen table—

but she was also aware that she might not have time. In this small plaza containing only a supermarket, a dry cleaner, and a coffee shop, the cake owner had probably only popped in to drop off shirts or pick up a latte, and would be back out at any moment. She put the cake on the front seat of her own car, then made haste to pull out of her spot, so she wouldn't still be there when the rightful owner returned from whatever errand she'd run after picking up the cake.

It turned out to be chocolate, typically her favorite, but it didn't taste as good as she'd hoped. This may have had something to do with the fact that she ate it too fast, sitting behind the steering wheel after she parked at work, and used the comb from her purse as a utensil, the closest thing to a fork she could find.

Gone it was, or nearly, when she clicked the plastic cover back onto the plastic plate, then shoved it onto the floor mat of her own passenger side. She arranged her sweater over it, so no one could look in and see what she'd done. As a cake, it had been on the small side, six inches around, but still. Obviously, the intention had been for at least three people to share it: the one the inscription referred to as "honey," and the two or more people who made up the "we." She scraped the corners of her lips clean with a pinky fingernail, looking into the rearview mirror, and left her lunch on the back seat.

She shivered all day in the air-conditioning, but would not let herself visit the lot to retrieve her sweater. A junior associate offered her his jacket as she led a meeting in the conference room, and when she thanked him and declined, he said, "But look—you have goose bumps!" He was not ordinarily a suck-up, so his solicitousness surprised her, and not in a comfortable way. On the way home she disposed of the remaining cake and its crumbs in a bin behind the Chinese restaurant she and her family often took out from. Then she drove to the front, went in through the door, and ordered dinner to bring home.

Her husband and children were happy to see her—or, it might more accurately be said, they were happy to see her carrying in food, because they knew that she knew precisely what to get for each of them, and they were all hungry.

For herself she had bought only a spring roll. "I had cake," she explained, and when her husband asked, "Whose birthday?," she gave him a smile and a shrug.

Everyone read their fortunes out loud. Her son and daughter, who were nine and eleven, got ones they didn't understand: *Fear is interest paid on a debt you may not owe. Land is always on the mind of a flying bird.* Her husband's said, *A good way to keep healthy is to eat more Chinese food,* and they all had a laugh over that.

She hoped they'd forget that she hadn't opened or read hers, but they didn't. She unrolled the slip slowly. *You are a closed book overdue to be opened.*

"That's true!" Her husband reacted with far more excitement than he should have, as if the fortune had put its finger on something he'd tried but failed to find words for. "They nailed you."

"*Bon appétit!*" said their daughter, who had recently taken to sprinkling French phrases into her speech. When they'd finished eating, the kids were excused to do their homework. "*À tout à l'heure,*" the girl told them before herding her brother upstairs.

Cate sat back in her chair. Her husband came over, put his hands on her shoulders, and began to rub. "You don't have to do that," she told him.

"But I want to. Doesn't it feel good?"

She wouldn't lie. "I love it. But that's enough, really." When he kept at it, even dug his hands in harder, she said, "Please, honey, stop."

He'd be hurt, she knew, so she didn't look at his face. He said, "Bad day, I take it?"

"Not bad enough."

She could tell he wanted to ask what she meant by this, but stopped himself. In the early days of their knowing each other, he delighted in the remarks of hers that would take him aback—spontaneous, silly things that either made no sense or made sense only to the two of them, so that their absurdity served to strengthen what was between them, as it excluded others from what they shared.

But this comment, about her day not having been bad enough—that did not bring them closer to each other at all.

In bed that night, turning over, she brushed his body by accident and apologized. "Please don't ever say you're sorry for touching me," he said. So she apologized for *that*. In the early days he would have laughed, they both would have, but they were beyond that now.

In the morning she reminded herself that it was a new day. She liked to do this sometimes, when she felt ashamed or guilty, when she knew she wasn't measuring up. That had been a favorite phrase of her mother's, *measuring up*, always in reference to someone failing or falling short; she would never have said, "You did a good job today, you really measured up."

Also in her head, as she dressed for work and ran through the day's obligations on her mental list, was another phrase, one she recalled from the church services she'd attended as a child. *This is the day the Lord hath made; rejoice and be glad in it!*

Even back then, so young, she'd loved the idea of each morning being a fresh, new chance. If you needed a do-over, here it was.

She did not feel capable of rejoicing or being glad, but she did try—and manage, somehow—to locate a fresh resolve to make this a better day than the one before. At work, she went out of her way to compliment everyone she encountered, whether they held positions above, below, or equal to her own. Only doing this did she realize that it was not her habit; she tended, without realizing (or did she realize and just not want to admit it?), to pay better attention to her superiors, though there were fewer of them than her subordinates. Acknowledging this to herself did not make her feel good, though correcting it did. The praise she gave was about the way they performed their jobs, not a tie they wore or a haircut they'd gotten. She'd read somewhere that this was the way to go: mention something specific you admire about a task they've performed. They feel seen that way. Appreciated.

And was it her imagination, or did everyone respond to her in kind? *That was a great memo you sent to Corporate. Thanks for the heads-up on the new deadline. Fantastic pitch.*

And so it was that she felt giddy, suffused with love, returning home. The kids were still at their after-school programs; her husband would pick them up on his way from work. She went online and searched for "Russian writer sugar bowl," and felt an unexpected lift when she saw the screen fill with links. But before she could click on any, the doorbell rang.

How did she know that it was something to be nervous about, and not merely a delivery or a solicitation? Somehow she did, feeling dread as she approached the door. When she saw a uniformed policeman on the other side, she thought, *Somebody's dead*, and immediately she understood she was being punished. Not for the cake, of course (she'd almost allowed herself to forget about that), but for all the other ways in which she hadn't measured up.

"What happened? Who?" she said before the officer could even confirm her identity. Once he did so, he hastened to tell her that it was nothing serious, nobody was hurt, he just had a few questions and would like to come in, if she didn't mind.

The relief she felt was so great that for a moment she thought she'd had an orgasm. Then she realized, no. But close. She ushered him inside and then had to sit down, because she was weak in the knees.

The officer was a young man, acne-pocked, who told her he was following up on a report. He shifted on the sofa, and she sensed his reluctance to say more. Finally, he mumbled that her license plate had shown up on a surveillance video. Yesterday morning, in the parking lot at Blue Ribbon Plaza; it showed a woman entering another car, removing something from it, transferring it to her own car, and driving away. "You couldn't tell from the video what the item was," he said. Now he was downright blushing, through the zit scars, at what he was about to accuse her of. "But we received a report about a stolen cake."

For a moment, Cate felt confused. Not because she wondered if her own actions had been real or only a dream, but because she couldn't imagine someone had actually reported to the police the theft of a cake that had cost a piddly $8.99. (Yes, she had made a note of the sticker price.)

Then she remembered that the person who deserved derision in this situation was herself, not whoever had reported being stolen from.

"Would that have been you?" the officer asked. His tone was afraid and gentle, which only made things worse.

She nodded. She tried to keep her head up, but it was impossible not to slouch.

"Well, the good news is they don't want to press charges. They just wanted me to ask—they just want to know—why? How does a person do something like that?"

For the rest of her life she would remember this question, and what he looked like when he asked it: fascinated, repulsed, even sympathetic, somehow all at the same time.

"It's complicated," she said, only then remembering that this was the catchphrase people were using now to describe relationships they didn't care to define further. "But I'm not a criminal," she added, realizing even as she spoke that the officer's very presence in her house indicated otherwise.

He waited. She was impressed that the young man didn't fidget or blink. She understood that the next line in this dialogue also belonged to her; she was supposed to insert an explanation, but her mind was a tangle of weeds and a substance she couldn't identify, something sticky that bound the weeds together and threatened to choke or drown them.

Though he wasn't obliged, the officer waded in there with her. "I had an uncle who was a drunk," he said in an uncertain but hopeful voice. "He managed to stay sober for a year once, but then he went back. He said he couldn't handle the pressure of acting like one kind of person when he felt like the exact opposite kind."

She hadn't imagined the weeds could constrict further, but they did. What gave him the right to talk to her about his uncle the drunk?

"He said it was a relief to get it over with. To prove he was the kind of person he felt like he was. Then he didn't have to wonder, or worry about it anymore."

This boy was half her age, she reminded herself, wearing a uniform that looked on him like a Halloween costume. "That's a sad story," she said. "But, you must realize, it has nothing to do with me." Immediately the weeds relaxed, and she could breathe again. She asked, "Did they happen to mention what the cake was for?"

Now he did blink, twice, and she was almost sorry to see she'd succeeded in sowing a marsh inside *him*. He fidgeted and said, "Yes, actually, they did." He'd been looking at her, but now he looked down at his shoes. "The woman bought it to congratulate her son for joining the JV tennis team."

Cate waited, until she realized that that was it. The cake had been intended to mark not a significant milestone or victory, but merely the kid's attachment to a team that probably, knowing this town, took anyone who wanted to play.

"Wow," she said, hoping he would not sense the sarcasm she felt but did not intend to communicate. "Well, that's sweet."

The officer stood, seeming to realize that the mission he'd set out on—to find out why a person of her obvious means and standing had stolen a cheap cake clearly intended to celebrate someone else—was a doomed one.

"Wait, please," she said, turning up to him the expression she was well aware tended to work the best, both at home and in the world. "I know you have no reason to believe me, but I don't go around doing things like this. It's . . . erratic, I know! I can't explain what came over me. I've been under a lot of pressure, and I guess it just got to a point . . ."

But he was not about to believe her. No doubt he saw her as a serial cake thief. (The notion of such a thing almost caused her to smile, but she caught it in time.) *Bat-shit crazy*, he was probably thinking. Or maybe he'd be more generous about it: *Eccentric. Unhinged.* Well, there was nothing to be done about that.

She told him, "I'd like to apologize, if I could. To the family. The mother. Can you tell me who they are?"

He shook his head and said he was afraid he couldn't give her that information. Was she wrong, or did he take a measure of satisfaction in telling her this? She knew she was not wrong.

A movement under her breastbone she recognized: the first stir of panic. "But why?"

"Confidentiality." He shrugged, and now there could be no denying the pleasure in his eyes.

"Oh." A gush of relief. "So, then, they don't know who I am?"

"It doesn't work that way. They have access to the full police report so, yes, they'll know *your* name."

She wanted to cry out, "That's not fair!" but she held her tongue, aware that if she protested, he might go on to use the words *victim* and *perpetrator*, and these she could not bear.

He said he was sorry as he preceded her to the door. On the porch, she saw, he noticed how beautiful her house looked—how vibrant the hanging flowerpots, how plush the cushioned wicker chairs. It did not bring her the comfort it usually did to watch her home being admired. As he walked toward the police car, she hoped he might wave, but he got in without turning, and without another word.

She sat again and began pressing her fingers into her face. She had a name in this town, she and her family did, and it was hardly possible that the mother of a child only slightly older than her own—the tennis player—would not recognize it upon reading it in the police report.

No, no, no. She could not allow these circumstances to stand. Didn't there have to be a way she could learn whose cake it had been, go to see the woman, and laughingly confess that she'd suffered an episode of some kind—medical, whatever—a bad reaction to a new medication, something that might make sense about why she had taken the cake?

There is always a solution, she was famous for saying at work.

But she would not find a solution to this one. She could think of no way out; a dozen kids had been named to the JV tennis team (that much she learned with a minimum of digging), and there was no way for her to guess whose celebration she had intruded upon. She imagined the mother, whoever she was—the cake buyer, the son celebrator, the Russian-short-story reader—telling her own friends, friends they inevitably shared, the bizarre story about the cake being stolen . . . and *guess who* the culprit had been?

And the children! It would affect them, too. No matter how much of a *petit secret* their friends' parents might try to keep it among the adults, it would get back to her son and daughter; of that there could be no doubt.

By the time her husband and the kids got home, she'd resolved what she had to do. For the rest of the evening, she gave them her best, lightest-hearted self. The next morning at the office, she contacted her company's headquarters in Trenton and told the person who'd approached her nearly a year ago that she was, in fact, interested in the position he had offered to create for her then. By the end of the day, they'd sketched out a preliminary deal. By the time she and her husband turned their lamps out that night before sleep, he'd agreed to think about the move, though the look on his face before the room went dark was one she'd hoped never to see again.

"What?" Cate said.

"I thought we'd decided to stay put here. I thought we agreed it was more important to give the kids some stability than to keep pushing ahead with our careers."

"It'll be fine. They'll love it. Besides, it's good for them— it teaches them how to adapt. Be resilient."

"They're already resilient. Haven't they been tested enough? And I thought you'd made some friends here. People you don't want to leave."

"Well. People are replaceable." When he flinched, she rushed to add, "I mean in the *friend* category. I can make new friends."

Dodie—that's who he was talking about. Her friend Dodie, from down the block: gap-toothed, sweat-panted, unsalaried, guffawing, generous, loving, irreplaceable Dodie.

Wasn't it possible—wasn't it just—that if she asked Dodie to go for one of their after-dinner walks, she could bring up the subject of the stolen cake in such a way that her friend would not only sympathize, but laugh, and even encourage Cate to laugh at herself? And then say, *You think that's bad? Listen to what* I *did once!*—after which they'd trade more stories and laugh some more, lose track of time, and have to be texted by their families before they remembered to return home?

It was tempting to believe. But in the end, she recognized a fantasy when she saw one.

Her husband said, "If we move there, that's where I'm staying. I'm staying put."

She promised quickly, ardently, then reached into his shorts. The next day she held her breath when the kids came home from school, but nothing appeared to have spoiled their natural cheer—until she and her husband sat them down and told them about the move. "But my team!" their daughter cried. "What about Sectionals? How am I supposed to tell Mr. Fritts? And—wait—*Ophelia!*" It was the name of her best friend that broke the dam holding back her tears. "You can't make me go." She would not be consoled. Their son did the opposite, as usual, and went silent.

"They'll be okay," her husband said, when he saw how much their reaction upset Cate.

And he was right. The following day, her son was already talking about going to Jets games and her daughter had identified the gymnastics school she wanted to attend in the suburb they'd targeted as their new home. After dinner that night, they told her to remain at the table as they banned her from the kitchen, and she heard giggling through the closed door. Then out came the three of them with her daughter leading, carrying a chocolate cake, which she almost dropped before her mother caught it and set it on the table. *Congratulations, Mommy!* it read across the top, squeezed out by some bakery employee in elegant iced cursive.

She smiled as much as she could and stood to kiss them. "Are those tears?" her husband asked. "Hey, look, guys, we made her cry."

"*Bon voyage* to us!" her daughter said. "Mommy, I'm sorry I was so mean."

They'd carried four plates and four forks out, and her husband set about cutting. He tried to hand her the first piece, but she shook her head and said, "You guys go ahead."

She knew she was supposed to take a slice and enjoy; the celebration, after all, was for her. "You don't want any?" her son asked, looking disappointed, and she told him, "Maybe later."

But they were voracious, her family. They dug in happily; they ate with the exuberant appetites of people about to set out on an adventure they hadn't anticipated and could not wait to begin. The cake was on the small side, six inches. As they ate and ate, it became apparent to each of them what they could only barely bring themselves to acknowledge, though Cate more than the rest: despite what the whole family hoped and in that moment intended, the three of them were going to finish it without her.

SKY HARBOR

She knew that none of her fellow passengers on this flight to Phoenix would have any idea what kind of journey she was embarking upon. If they bothered to guess, they might get part of it right: a grandmother—traveling alone, so probably widowed—on her way to visit grandchildren who lived across the country. This was all true. It was the part she admitted to her seatmate, a flushed and swollen woman in her middle thirties who ordered two Bloody Mary mixes with her tomato juice, when it wasn't even noon yet in any of the time zones they would inhabit during the flight. The woman was on her way to see her sister in a desert rehab facility favored by celebrities. "She was always the wild one," the woman told Helen, not seeming to notice the peanuts that fell out of her clenched fist and into her blouse. "Just because I'm older doesn't mean I could have done anything about it—it's not my fault."

"I'm going to see my son and his family," Helen said. "They live near Camelback." When Ethan and Sandra had moved there twelve years earlier, Helen and Bob kept up with them on a hike to the top of the mountain (Helen had thought she would be the one to slow down the excursion, but it was Bob who stumbled, twice on the rocky climb, and wouldn't let Helen shout ahead to alert Ethan and Sandra), and then they all celebrated by going out for Mexican food. Helen and Ethan and Bob ordered margaritas, and after Sandra smiled at them while asking the waitress for a seltzer, she and Ethan broke the news that she was pregnant. Helen remembered the expression on her son's face as he reached for his wife's hand and let her say the actual words. He looked the same way he had on his first day of kindergarten, when all the kids stood outside the classroom door with their mothers, waiting for the teacher to call their names, at which point they crossed the threshold and went inside to begin school. At both moments, his face betrayed the belief that he might not be able to bear the weight of the emotions the occasion required of him.

But he had; he had borne them. And much more, Helen knew, even though she had not been present at her grand-daughter's birth, or at her grandson's, or at the moment Ethan received Helen's own phone call notifying him of his father's death. She had not been present when the doctor summoned Ethan and Sandra into his office to explain what was happening in Ethan's bloodstream, what they could do for him, and for how long. Though she would not dare confess it to anyone, Helen was ashamed to feel glad she had not been there for that appointment. She was quite sure she would have failed to manage it. She had no idea how she was going to manage the trip she was making now, which was not in fact a visit, but something else.

Reaching under the seat in front of her, she lifted from her purse the notebook she'd dug out from the box beneath her bed, when it became clear that today was imminent. She opened it to the first page, which was blank despite her previous efforts to come up what she should put there—what she should outline, and maybe even rehearse, in the hope of saying the right thing when the time came.

You say so many things to your children. How many words, over the years—a million? She had never been good at estimates or calculations. But whatever the count, she knew that most of what she'd said to Ethan had not been important. She understood that now. The page remained blank in front of her.

"She doesn't know I'm coming," the woman next to her mumbled as they began their descent. Helen had thought she was asleep. "If she tells me to fuck off, I will—I'll get on the next plane back. I'm her sister, not her mother. Why do I need to put myself through that?"

Sandra and Robert picked her up at Sky Harbor. Helen almost didn't recognize her daughter-in-law, though it had been only a month and a half since she'd seen her last. "I know it's a cliché for people's hair to go white when they're scared," Sandra said, trying to laugh as she hugged Helen in greeting. "But really it's been this way for years. Or would have been. I haven't made it to the hairdresser this summer—I just can't see the point."

As they pulled out of the airport parking lot, she told Helen that Cadence was at the hospital with Ethan, reading to her father from the novel she was writing.

"Novel?" Helen said. Her granddaughter was eleven.

Sandra smiled, at least with her lips, in the driver's seat next to Helen. Behind them, Robert leaned forward and said to his grandmother, "I've read it. It's good, actually. It's about a girl who can make anything she wants happen, just by wishing for the opposite thing."

"That happens to me all the time," Helen said, but neither of them seemed to realize she was trying to set up a joke. "For instance, I asked for a window seat on the plane today, but instead I got the aisle." Though she knew it was what the kids would call *lame*, she felt giddy with the desire to make everyone feel better, so she continued, "I asked for nice grandchildren, but instead I got you and Cadence. I asked for—" But her voice faltered without her realizing it was going to, and she faked a cough, as if that was what caused her to stop speaking.

In Ethan's hospital room, Cadence and her father

were both asleep—he in his bed, she in the vinyl puke-colored chair pulled up close to Ethan's side. (During Ethan's first treatment, the kids had gotten a lot of mileage out of Robert's adjective for the chair's color, but that felt like a long time ago.) The notebook Cadence was writing the novel in was not unlike the notebook Helen carried in her purse; it had fallen to the floor, and Helen picked it up to read the opening aloud. "*What a gorges day, she thought as the sun peaked through the window. I wonder whats going to happen next?*" Her voice woke Cadence, and she blinked a few times before getting up to hug her grandmother. She'd always slept hard, particularly as an infant. Once when Helen and Bob were babysitting during a Christmas visit, he'd gone in to get her up from her crib because he thought she was napping too long, and when he couldn't rouse her, he panicked and called Helen in, sure that the baby was dead. Helen rushed in with alarm in her heart, but not because she thought Bob was right; she'd fallen asleep, which she'd promised herself she wouldn't do until Ethan and Sandra got home. Cadence woke up and started crying at all the commotion, and she was still crying when her parents returned. Helen and Bob never told them why, because Bob was embarrassed that he hadn't known better, so the story was Helen's alone now. "I like your novel," Helen told Cadence. "I only read the first two sentences. But Robert told me what it was about."

Her granddaughter shrugged. It was a gesture intended to convey that she could take or leave the compliment, but Helen saw she was pleased. "How's your dad?" she asked, and Cadence seemed only then to remember where they all were, and why.

"He's good. I mean, not *good*. You know what I mean. But at least he makes sense today."

"It's the drugs," Sandra explained to Helen. "They make him go in and out. He sees things that aren't there—he sees *people.* The other day he had a whole conversation with some-one named Yola. Does that name mean anything to you?"

Helen cried, "That was his old piano teacher—his first!" Then she needed to press her hand into her chest to keep it from moving too hard at the memory, those determined little fingers cupped over the keys.

"Oh," Sandra said. "That's right; he told me that once. I'd forgotten. Anyway, it's not always like that. Sometimes he's lucid." She turned to her son and daughter. "When he wakes up, I'm taking you guys home for a while, and Grandma can stay with him." She said it firmly, as if she expected the children might object, but both of them appeared to brighten at the prospect of being able to leave the hospital room. It struck Helen that this was not how they should be spending their summer, while their friends splashed around in pools and ate ice cream.

"Maybe you could all go to a movie or something," she suggested to Sandra. Robert's eyes lit up, but then he saw his mother and sister looking at Helen with the condescending pity reserved for someone who was—as she knew the kids would say—totally clueless, and he arranged his own features to mirror theirs.

Alone with her son after the nurse had come in to check on things, Helen moved the chair a bit back from the bed, so she could see him better. "Not exactly my idea of a summer vacation," she told him. "I don't appreciate this one bit."

"You'll get over it." Ethan's voice held the laughter he would have let out if he'd been able, and Helen rushed to supply it for them both. It had been one of Bob's favorite phrases, and it was always a secret unfunny joke between Helen and Ethan, because Bob said it regardless of how likely it was that the person in question might actually "get over it." He said it when Helen lost the second and third pregnancies to miscarriage. He said it when Ethan didn't make the basketball team that supposedly took everybody who wanted to play. He said it when the stories about him in the local newspaper made his wife and son afraid to go out of the house and be recognized. For all Helen knew, he might even have said it now.

"What do you think?" she asked her son. She knew she did not have to elaborate; Ethan would understand what she meant.

Against the pillow he tried to shrug, but she could tell that a pain shot through him halfway into the motion, so he stopped. "Maybe a day or two," he told her. "Maybe less. It's weird, Mom. I can feel it."

They had always been able to talk this way. It made things both better and worse in the present circumstance. "Don't feel like you have to keep me company," she said as Ethan struggled to keep his eyes open, and in the wake of her reassurance, he slept again.

Six o'clock in the evening. Sandra had said she'd return with the kids by eight. Helen got up and looked out the window. The vegetation on the rise above the hospital was still unfamiliar to her, though during her visits to the Southwest over the years, they had all tried to teach her the names of the various cactus types—*wolf's cholla, organ pipe, saguaro.* The last one, she did recognize. It looked like a man standing with his arms raised to either side of his body, lifting them toward the sky in supplication. She looked at the tallest one for a long time until she heard her son's voice behind her, asking a question it took her a moment to ascertain.

"Do you think there's anything out there?" At first she thought he was referring to the landscape beyond the window. Then she realized that he meant heaven, or God. She had not expected this question from him, and she had not prepared an answer.

She urged herself to just tell him the truth, but when she opened her mouth, she found—to her own surprise and chagrin—that she wasn't sure what the truth would be. "Sometimes," she said to Ethan, and he looked disappointed by her reply.

"But you don't think I'm going to run into Dad or anything, right?"

"Well, if you do, you'll get over it." She knew as soon as she said it that it had been a mistake. The time for jokes was over. He'd seen this before she did.

"Mom," Ethan said, and when his voice split on the word, as it had when he was an adolescent, she held up the cup of water so he could sip from the straw. He swallowed in jerks, then had to take a moment to recover. Helen fought the impulse to look away as he summoned all of his energy to ask, "Do you think he did it, or not?" before falling back against the pillow.

She did her best not to choke on the shock. She'd thought that they were beyond this, too: that question. It had not occurred to her, flying out here, that in his condition and with the time he had left, Ethan might ask her whether she believed his father had committed the crime he'd gone to prison for.

She'd expected it back then, beginning the night before Bob reported to the Fishkill Correctional Facility, in Ethan's last month of eighth grade. They sat their son down, and Bob did the talking, as they had agreed. He had no idea why the girl's mother would say what she did, he told Ethan. He had no previous record of such behavior, and it didn't make sense that in his position as a school administrator, with so much to lose through such an indiscretion, he would start now. These were pretty much the same words his lawyer had used in court.

People didn't like that he used the word *indiscretion*.

"Sexual touching of a child is not an 'indiscretion,'" read a piece on the Op-Ed page of the local newspaper. "The charges involve a six-year-old. It is an offense and a crime.

"He'd be more outraged if he were innocent," the editorial continued. "Robert Metzger's demeanor is one of a man who has been found out."

Though Helen tried to ignore it, the last lines stuck in her mind like a mantra she had not invited, which she found herself unable to shake. She could not imagine exhibiting the calmness Bob displayed, let alone feeling it, in the face of being accused of something atrocious and shameful she hadn't done. Also, he had refused to testify, which she did not understand even when he tried to explain it to her. ("I'm not refusing, I'm declining. There's a difference. I'm declining to dignify this trial by participating in any way."). Bob told her that since *he* knew the truth, as of course she and Ethan did, that was all that mattered. The stance all three of them took, both within and outside the family, was that they had been wronged. Though Helen wanted desperately to move to another town—if not to another state—because of the way everyone treated her and Ethan during that time (they both grew used to feeling either invisible or like criminals themselves; though she would not have guessed it beforehand, invisible was worse), Bob said he understood but he begged her not to leave, reminding her during one of their early visits together that it would only make people more certain that his conviction had been just.

During the two years Bob was in jail, she waited for Ethan to ask whether she believed his father was guilty. Dreading the question, she thought she might be able to answer if she wrote down all the possible permutations of a response in the notebook she'd bought when it caught her eye in Walgreens the day she stopped to pick up the medicine she took briefly, after Bob went to prison, in an effort to feel happier—until she realized that there was good reason *not* to feel happy, her mind and her body were reacting in exactly the right ways to her circumstance, and she stopped taking the pills. But she'd kept the notebook. She thought that if she wrote enough, someday it might appear on the page by accident—the answer—in the same way she'd heard once that if a bunch of monkeys were placed in a room filled with typewriters, eventually one of them would reproduce the entire works of Shakespeare.

But she never wrote anything, and Ethan never asked her, even on their drives to and from the correctional facility, which looked like a cross between a monastery and one of those old resorts in the Catskills—sprawling, on a hill, with turrets. Ethan had planned to accompany Helen on her first visit after Bob's conviction, but as they approached the prison, he changed his mind. "I'm sure it's not all that bad inside," Helen told him, but her son shook his head and said it wasn't that—it wasn't how it looked that skeeved him out—but he'd done some research on the place and learned that it had begun as a hospital for the criminally insane. For the *furiously mad*. "Did you know that, Mom?" he asked.

She had not. For a few moments, hearing it, she'd been tempted to turn around and drive them both back home. Bob was expecting them, though; and not only that, she knew she couldn't put it off forever. Ethan said he'd wait in the car, but then across the highway they noticed a pop-up carnival advertising a Gravitron and a Whip and a Freefall, and she dropped him off there instead.

If Bob was surprised or hurt or both that his son had not come to see him, he didn't show it, and Helen remembered only then something he'd told her once about cats: as their species evolved, they learned that it was to their benefit not to signal any distress. She and her husband spoke about things (anything either of them could think of) other than

Julie Coyle. He told her the older inmates said the prison was haunted by ghosts, the tormented souls of those who'd died in the building when it was an asylum. She searched his face for signs of amusement, but saw none. "You don't believe that, though, right?" she asked—there could have been no bigger skeptic than her husband about the mystic or supernatural. He shrugged and smiled and said, "Of course not," but not before she'd seen something cross his face she didn't recognize, something that caused her to question further whether she knew him as well as she'd thought she did.

When she picked Ethan up from the carnival afterward, he told her he'd thrown up twice. Helen did not confide in him that she'd vomited, too, in the skeevy ladies' lavatory before she forced herself to calm down, for Bob's sake more than her own. The sight of him smiling at her as she entered the visiting room had caused her stomach to flip again, but she was pretty sure she managed to hide it. *I can be like a cat, too*, she'd thought.

When the carnival shut down at the end of October, Ethan agreed to go inside the prison with Helen. But he never asked his father if he was guilty. Nor did he ask him in all the years during which Bob came home to live with them again and Ethan went off to college, graduated, married, and moved away. Helen knew this because Bob told her in a tone of pride, the source of which was his assumption that his son did not have to ask, because he knew his father could not possibly have done what he'd been accused of.

When Bob returned to them, he began seeing a therapist as ordered by the court. He never told Helen what they talked about in his sessions, which he attended every week until he died the year before their grandson was born. As a new widow, Helen made several appointments with the same man, hoping she'd be able to learn something from him—the most crucial thing— about her husband. During her last session, she confessed that she thought it was possible her husband had fondled Julie Coyle.

And if she thought it was possible, she asked the therapist, what did this say about her marriage? What did it say about her? Though the therapist made it clear that he could not in good conscience betray a dead man's confidence, when he responded to her questions by shifting and clearing his throat, she interpreted it as confirmation of her suspicions. She never went back.

In Ethan's hospital room, she let her eyes flick again toward the window and sent a quick prayer to the saguaro, because she didn't know what her answer should be. She had never lied to her son (unless you counted Santa Claus, which she did not), and she would have liked to have shared it with him—this burden. He was the only one in the world who would understand.

But what did it mean that she would even consider sending her son out of the life she'd born him to, with such a thorn lodged in his heart? How could that be the right thing to do? It was possible, she thought, that even the way Ethan had equivocated in the question was his way of letting her know what he needed from her.

She turned back to him from the window, hoping he'd fallen asleep. But he was staring at her with an intensity she hadn't seen since before he got sick, waiting for her answer. Then she couldn't resist, or as she would think so often later, she *didn't* resist; the anticipation of the relief she knew she'd feel, being able to say it—finally, to the one other person who had lived it, too—overwhelmed her. She told herself that acknowledging what she was sure they must both believe would relieve him as much as it would her. "I think he might have, honey," she said to her son, and only in the next moment, seeing his face, did she understand what a miscalculation she had made.

When he fell under the drugs again, she tried to get comfortable in the puke-colored chair. A nurse came in to adjust something in Ethan's IV, which she promised she could do without waking him. Helen took her purse and went down the hall to the cafeteria, which was practically empty at this time of night. There were two young women, whom Helen took from their white coats and dazed expressions to be doctors at the end of their shift, sitting across from each other at a table by the window and pulling French fries from a plate on the tray between them. They didn't speak or look out the window, through which Helen made out the same saguaro she'd seen from Ethan's room.

Helen approached the counter, where another woman in a different white uniform told her that the grill was closed, but that she could take any of the wrapped plates she wanted from the crisper. She hadn't eaten anything since the peanuts on the plane, and although she suspected that she wasn't supposed to be hungry—because of grief—she was. Down the railing she slid her tray carrying a tuna sandwich with chips, and when she reached the register, she asked the woman for a soda.

"It's free," the woman told her, and when Helen didn't understand at first, she repeated, "It's free. The food. They don't charge for it after seven thirty."

She mumbled a thank-you and carried the tray to a table, where she pulled out a chair and sat down, intending to eat. Almost as soon as she unwrapped the sandwich, she realized that not having had to pay for it made her not want it anymore.

When she returned to the room, Sandra had come back with the children, and Helen tried not to notice that her daughter-in-law disapproved of her having left Ethan alone. His breath-

167

ing had progressed to the agonal stage, and hearing the nurse say the word *agonal* made Helen flinch to such a degree that Sandra put her arms out, as if afraid Helen might collapse. He died two hours later. One of the two dazed-looking women doctors she had seen eating French fries came in to declare the death. Helen saw a smear of ketchup on the doctor's coat sleeve, and this, after everything, was what made her stumble, cry out, and reach for the chair. When they finally had to leave, Cadence kicked her notebook under the bed and said she was never writing a stupid fucking novel again. Helen got down on her hands and knees to retrieve it, but she knew better than to offer the book to her granddaughter. "I'll keep it in case you ever want it back," she said, and it was only then that Cadence began to wail.

It didn't matter now—what she had said to Ethan. Did it matter? Of course it mattered, but Helen had not been able to figure out yet, exactly, *how*. She had been back, in her life in the East, for a month after her son died, when she awoke one morning from a dream featuring a landscape she'd inhabited as a child. Her grandparents had owned a cottage situated on a bluff overlooking a small lake in the Helderberg Mountains outside Albany, and on weekends in the summer Helen and her mother made the forty-five-minute drive north to where the air always held at least a slight chill, even on the hottest days. This was because the lake was surrounded by old, high trees that blocked and blunted the sun, except as it beat down directly on the water itself. Though she knew how to swim, she hesitated to do so in the lake, because of the squishy bottom. Her grandfather would stand in a spot just beyond the dock and try to coax her out. "There's a stone in here somewhere with your name on it," he'd tell her. "Don't you want to come out to see for yourself?" In her younger years, she believed he meant a stone that literally contained the letters spelling *Helen*, even though her grandmother always chided him by saying "Henry, that isn't nice."

He also told her that if she kept swimming, she'd eventually come to a warm spot, which *was* true, and which almost made it worth it.

Her family always emphasized the word *cottage* when they talked about their summer place, to distinguish it from the three-story A-frame across the lake which they called, derisively, The Estate. The inhabitants of The Estate seemed to host parties every weekend, sending toward Helen's grandparents' dock all kinds of raucous noise and tumbling wakes from their motorboat joyrides along the length of the lake. Her grandparents and her mother never said anything, in keeping with their professed opinion that people should live and let live, but it was easy for Helen to sense their irritation and their distaste.

And for this reason, she could not tell them that she was intrigued by The Estate and jealous of those who lived or visited there, especially the children. From the dock off the cottage she watched their figures jump and dive from their own longer, wider dock across the way, splashing one another or playing Marco Polo or paddling out to the laddered swim raft a hundred yards from the shore. The sun always seemed to be sparkling throughout the big house itself, reflecting off the windows that made up the entire lakeside wall.

Once, she thought she heard a girl about her own age call out to people on the beach behind her that she was going to do handstands in the water, and that she wanted them to time how long she could hold her breath. Helen was so squeamish about her feet touching the bottom that she couldn't imagine putting her hands down there, and she peered as closely as she could across the lake to get a better view of whoever it was who was brave enough to do this, but she could only make out three or four girls laughing together as they laid their towels down, and it could have been any one of them.

Occasionally, Helen would hear a swear from the other side: "Goddamn this fucking thing!" when a motor wouldn't start, or "Eat them raw for all I care, I don't give a shit." When the kids of The Estate became teenagers like Helen herself, she caught in the air on the dock one day the smell of pot, and she could tell from the way her mother and grandparents looked up and sniffed that they smelled it, too, though none of them said anything.

And on one Fourth of July, she happened to be staring across the water when the girl she had identified as being closest to her own age flounced down the lawn to The Estate's dock, pulled her T-shirt over her head, and lay on a chaise with her face lifted toward the sun. As she leaned back, Helen saw the flash of two small white globes of flesh that looked exactly like the ones lately protruding from her own chest, and she managed to hold back a gasp.

It would not have done, in any way, to tell the grown-ups what was going on across the lake. Her grandparents in particular were doing their best, she knew, to instill in her the values they themselves prescribed, the values exemplified by their bias toward *cottage* over *estate*: reticence, modesty, moral rectitude. They weren't words Helen thought at the time, but later when she learned them all, she conjured her grandparents' faces. Their voices saying things like, *If you always tell the truth, you never have to worry about being caught in a lie,* or, *You can't make the same mistake twice because the second time it's not a mistake—it's a choice.*

But hold on. Was it a mistake or a choice or something else when her grandfather, later that same summer, began bringing his binoculars down to the dock? Before then, when he wasn't wearing them around his neck during their bird-watching walks, he always kept them in their case on the table at the side of his chair on the sunporch. When Helen's grandmother shifted her lawn chair on the dock, almost setting the legs on the binoculars, and he yelled at her to be careful and she yelled back, "What are those doing down here?" he said he thought he'd seen a great blue heron and wanted to have the glasses on hand if it came round again.

And what was Helen's grandmother choosing when she only pursed her lips at hearing this, muttered, "There aren't any blue herons around here, great or otherwise," picked up her chair, and moved it a foot or two away from her husband?

These weren't questions Helen asked herself at the time, of course. But later. When it was too late.

The motorboats from The Estate didn't usually get going until after lunchtime, so on Saturday mornings Helen passed the hours floating on the patched blue raft her grandfather dragged up for her each week from the cottage's basement, over the cement steps, and out the flimsy bulkhead doors she'd learned to stay away from, and fear, because, when she was seven she'd climbed on top one day trying to get a better look at a hummingbird, then fell through the doors when they gave way under her weight.

During that fall, in less than a second's worth of time, she experienced her first mature complexity of emotions: terror at the idea that she was about to die—that all of this was going to be over far more abruptly than she had ever guessed; exhilaration because, at the age of seven, something dramatic and remarkable was finally happening to her; and worst of all, disappointment at recognizing that if she *did* die, as she expected to, she would miss witnessing the reactions of other people to her death. When she landed half on her back, half on her butt on the cellar's soft dirt floor, she didn't understand at first that she was still alive. She knew she would always remember those moments, though she never articulated these nuanced insights to herself or anyone else. Of course, surviving turned out to be not nearly as momentous or rewarding as, during the fall, she'd imagined it would be.

By nature, she was a cautious child. She was always checking—her mother's face, the clock on the wall, her own mouth in the mirror—for signs that things were not as they should be: anxiety, tardiness, crumbs. The first few times she lay on the raft and kicked herself gently away from the dock, smelling comfort in the blue rubber and hearing the sharp call of loons, she dared to close her eyes and feel the not-unpleasant sense of suspension this temporary blindness afforded her, but she always opened her eyes again within a few seconds, afraid that she had floated too far away, off-course, while choosing irresponsibly to let her awareness stray.

One day during the summer she saw the first and only topless sunbather of her life, she lay on the raft with her eyes closed and wondered what would be the worst thing that could happen, if she decided not to open them—not to check. The lake was small, she reasoned. Though she was worried by the buoys scattered across the surface, her grand-father had assured her that the hazards they signaled, such as tree stumps, were only for the occasional speedboat. She'd never found, upon opening her eyes, that she was anywhere other than where she expected to be. She knew how to swim, there was no current, and either her mother or one of her grandparents—and often all three—were sitting on the dock when she set out, watching over her; if she were ever to approach any danger, they would call a warning or, if it came to that, save her. She began testing it, leaving her eyes closed for longer and longer intervals, discovering how delicious it was to feel awake and asleep at the same time.

Was there a part of her that wished she might float close enough to The Estate to get a good look at the people over there? In the manner of such things, she entertained the notion for only a moment before sending it away.

Once she actually *did* fall asleep, awakening when her foot grazed the exact spot she would have aimed for if she'd been trying—the post of the dock where her family sat with their sweating glasses of ice tea, welcoming her back to them and asking if she'd had fun. She still remembered, all these years later, the surprise and relief she'd felt upon realizing that everything was still all right, despite the fact that she'd let her vigilance go.

Other than those mornings on the raft before her grandparents died and her mother had to sell the cottage, the only time she had felt so safe—so free of the need to monitor what was going on around her—was the first stretch of her marriage to Bob, up until he was accused and convicted and sent away. And not since then.

In her dream after Ethan's death, lying on the blue raft as the child she had been, she woke up to find herself floating through a narrow rill that had not existed in the reality of her grandparents' land. The stream carried her to the ocean, where everything was the opposite of the scene she had just left; the sky was dark with rain clouds, the waves violent and high. They tossed her off the raft within seconds, and she plunged straight down through the gray water, to the cafeteria at the bottom of the sea. Able to breathe again, and to shake the seaweed out of her eyes, she chose her items and slid her tray down the rail to the cash register. "You don't have enough money," the cashier told her when Helen handed over the rung-up amount.

"It's right here," Helen said, pointing to the bills and change she had placed in the cashier's hand. "All of it. See?"

"It's not enough," the cashier insisted, shaking her head as if to let Helen know that she was accustomed to people trying to pull the wool over her eyes. She took Helen's tray and her money and dumped it all in the trash. Helen tried to protest that it wasn't fair, but before she could get the words out, she awoke to the room she had gone to sleep in, and the bed she had shared with Bob.

She expected the dream's ghost to haunt her all morning—it had been that vivid—so she was surprised when, by the time she finished her grapefruit, it had dissolved to vapor while she wasn't looking. Still, she wished it were a weekday, rather than Saturday, so she could go to work and lose herself in the tasks that had piled up on her desk while she'd been gone. What she liked most about her job was that the worst that could happen, if she made a mistake, was a delay in reimbursement to client institutions who'd already paid out on insurance claims. Nobody was going to suffer if Helen screwed up.

For this, she had Bob to thank. The occasion of their meeting was the job interview he conducted when she applied to teach second grade at his school. The job went to someone else, but shortly afterward he called to invite Helen to lunch. She was inclined to say no, but he said on the phone that he wanted to explain, so she agreed to meet him. The restaurant was one she'd never been to before, and she could see right away that it was the romantic sort: cozy booths separated into their own nooks, the window shades lowered halfway against the noon sun. Helen held herself stiffly, thinking as soon as she was seated that she shouldn't have come, but within a few minutes Bob had her laughing, even about the fact that he'd chosen someone else for the teaching job. Something she'd mentioned during the interview clued him in that she didn't really want it, he said. About how it had been her mother who suggested she get a teaching degree, when Helen herself had been set on finance. And if she didn't really want the job, it wouldn't serve his school to have her in it.

"Am I being presumptuous?" he asked then. "And will you forgive me?"

How dare you, she thought she should say, but in fact he was right; she herself hadn't even been aware of why she'd brought up the fact, during the interview, that she'd switched her major from business to education halfway through. Someone else might have called him on it, though. Might even have sued for what he'd told her. Why had he taken the risk? She could only conclude that he liked her—*like* liked her, as she'd heard other girls say. By dessert she'd confessed, "I do love kids, just not a whole bunch at once," and told him about the day during her student-teaching assignment that all the third-graders in her classroom had decided to imitate everything she did and said, to the point that she shut herself in the bathroom and cried. She'd never told anyone, because she felt so ashamed.

"You're sensitive," Bob told her. "Nothing wrong with that. But teachers need thicker skin."

It annoyed her to think that he might even after this short time know her better than she knew herself, and she told him so.

"Not at all." Was it possible he winced a little, hearing this? "Do you really think anyone can know us better than we know ourselves?" Then, seeming to realize he'd put her on the spot, he added, "To me it's more a question of *listening* to what we know. Paying attention. Following it."

They began dating and she went back to school to finish her business degree; it didn't fulfill her mother's vision of Helen working in a "helping profession," but by then Helen could ignore what her mother thought. She built a career she enjoyed because nothing gratified her more than to make all the numbers add up.

After she returned from Arizona, her company had offered her some time off—bereavement leave, the HR person called it—but Helen knew that time off was the last thing she needed. Too late, she realized that the time to have taken the leave was *before* Ethan died, so she could have spent those months out there with him and Sandra and the children. But she could only know this in retrospect, because at the time, she'd refused to believe it would end the way it did; she'd insisted to herself that he would get better. He had to. She couldn't conceive of the other thing.

She was supposed to be preparing to sell her house and make arrangements to move out to Phoenix, to be near Sandra and the kids. It was what they had talked about in the wake of Ethan's death; a few days after the funeral, Sandra even drove her around some "senior-centered" condo complexes, to show Helen what was available. Through her numbness, Helen recognized and appreciated the fact that her daughter-in-law and grandchildren really did seem to want her around, and weren't just suggesting the move for her sake. When she was out there, it made sense. But since she'd been back, the idea of leaving felt wrong. She hadn't contacted a realtor or given notice at her job. Even though she had come to hate northeastern winters, this was the place she knew.

And she had friends—people who'd come around, after Bob was released, to the notion that maybe someone who refused to take a plea deal *was* innocent, after all. If he'd been guilty, why not say so, serve a shorter sentence, and be home with his family all the sooner? Move away to a place where no one would know them, and start again?

Besides, it was all old news by now. The statute of limitations on the scandal seemed to have run out. Some people, new to the town, had never known about it. Others agreed, without exactly saying so, to forget.

The school district couldn't or wouldn't hire Bob back after he was released, but he'd gotten a job at an educational consulting company, where he worked without any problems for almost fifteen years—literally until the day he died, of a heart attack at an Outcomes Assessment conference in Indianapolis. ("What on earth is 'Outcomes Assessment'?"

Helen remembered asking, the morning he left, and when he explained that it had to do with measuring how well a school fulfilled its Student Learning Objectives, she groaned and said, "I can't imagine anything more boring.")

Helen's friends, some of them mothers of kids who'd gone to school with Ethan, were women she saw in her exercise class or at the Literary League she belonged to at the library, where a retired English professor, Enid Burkhard, led monthly discussions on novels and stories in translation. They were mostly classics from the nineteenth and twentieth centuries, but occasionally she threw in a contemporary book. Since Helen had begun attending, more than a year before Ethan first got diagnosed, her favorites had been *The Death of Ivan Ilyich* and *Madame Bovary*. Her friend Liane, who prided herself on being up on the latest lingo, called Enid a "Debbie Downer." But Helen liked reading about despair, regret, illness, and other obstacles the characters faced, which they found difficult or even impossible to overcome. The stories other people called "depressing" were the ones that made Helen feel both more alive and less alone.

She almost skipped the lecture scheduled for that afternoon, thinking she might follow her impulse to drive up to the lake cottage in the Helderbergs instead. It was the first week in March and the air felt freakishly warm, nearly sixty-five degrees before nine in the morning. Like everyone else, Helen knew it was only a fleeting reprieve.

Her mother had inherited the cabin from her parents when they died, but sold it shortly afterward to send Helen to college. Helen begged her not to do it, but her mother refused to let her take out a loan. The day before the deed traded hands, they drove up to the lake for a final visit, and walked together down the path toward the dock. Helen did her best not to cry as it occurred to her that she would never see these trees again, or the constellation of those sinister buoys, or the perfect circle of sunlight that fell at a certain time of day on the overturned canoe. Her mother opened her hand to show two small stones she'd picked up on the path without Helen's noticing. She told Helen to take one, then flung the remaining stone out over the water as far as she could. Helen did the same, trying to match the arc and distance of her mother's shot, even though she would have preferred to have a flatter stone to skip across the surface the way her grandfather had taught her (her record was seven skips). They heard the two small plinks, watching the tiny ripples vanish almost as soon as they appeared. "Now there'll always be a part of us here," her mother said, and she sounded so pleased by the thought that Helen did not offer her own opinion, which was that tossing a stone into the water was a meaningless gesture; the stone had nothing to do with her. "We're making a memory," her mother added, drawing Helen into a hug, and *this* pierced Helen so sharply that she couldn't help breaking down, even though she knew it would distress her mother enough to undo whatever consolation she'd taken in throwing her little rock.

Driving away from the cottage together for the last time, they said good-bye aloud to Beaver Shores Road, pretending they thought it was a silly thing to do. When her mother paused at the intersection, Helen said, "What happens if you go that way?" and pointed left. It was a question she'd asked her grandparents every time one of them was driving and they made the right-hand turn that would take them home along the route so familiar that she could tell where they were even with her eyes closed. In fact, she'd made a game of it over the years, closing her eyes, waiting, and picturing what she'd see out the window when she opened them again. She almost always nailed it within a matter of yards.

Her mother's answer was a version of the one her grand-parents had always given, along with the same gesture: a slight shrug as if to indicate it wasn't worth the bother. "Just the lake on the other side."

And as always, Helen did not follow up with the question she wished she could ask: "Don't you want to go see? What it's like over there?" because they were not that kind of people, her grandparents or her mother; unless there was some errand or appointment at your destination, there was no point in making the trip.

When she married Bob, she had not seen the cottage for ten years, since that day before the closing of the property's sale to a middle-aged widow named Jacqueline Witt. Helen's mother did not attend the closing, so Helen knew nothing about the new owner, other than her name, until her thirtieth birthday, when Bob told her that he couldn't wrap her present; they would have to drive to pick it up. Buckled into his booster seat in the back, Ethan, who was six and a new reader, sounded out every sign he saw along the highway.

Helen pretended not to have any idea where they were going, even though she'd understood immediately, the moment Bob took the ramp to head north, that he had arranged with Jacqueline Witt for Helen to see the cottage of her childhood. She would do that for her husband, she decided—show him the sidelong puzzled question in her eyes, which he must be waiting for, followed by a slow dawning, then delight. She would do it despite the fact that the feeling was not delight but dread; she did not want to go back. The cottage, as a memory, was perfect the way it was, even if you included the breathless backward fall through the bulkhead doors.

Arriving, they discovered that a tradition had sprung up since Helen's last time there. On Beaver Shores Road, owners had taken to posting wooden signs announcing names of their cabins, such as *License to Chill* and *Beachy Keen*. The one previously belonging to Helen's grandparents had been dubbed *Witt's End*. "You have to admit that's pretty clever," Bob said, and though Helen smiled and understood her own reaction to be ungracious and petty, she thought, *I don't have to admit anything.*

She'd worried that the cabin might have been left to deteriorate, after all this time. But instead a whole wing had been added, along with a wraparound deck. The exterior had been repainted, not long ago by the looks of it. Jacqueline Witt stood in the doorway, in the exact spot Helen's grandmother should have been, to welcome them. She wore her silver hair in a sophisticated, flyaway bob, and a scarf tied in a style that looked vaguely Parisian, though this was only the Helderbergs. She showed them around and enumerated the changes she'd made to the cabin—switched out the appliances, put in a gas line, winterized the three-season porch. The walls had been repaneled with knotty pine, and the ceiling raised to include rafters and a skylight. Drapes, two Duchamp prints, a decorative beam.

It was still a far cry from The Estate, but it occurred to Helen that her grandparents would not have recognized this place as the one they'd bought so many years ago. She closed her eyes briefly to picture them sitting on the dock together, side by side as always, as they worked duplicate copies of the same crossword puzzle—not competing against each other, but enjoying the shared challenge.

When Jacqueline saw Helen's reaction, she had the grace to say she hoped Helen approved. Would Ethan like a cookie? Yes, as it turned out, he would. Jacqueline set a plate of mint Milanos on the table, and they all sat down. "This place is beautiful," Bob said, and to Helen it sounded as if he were accusing her of always having downplayed her grandparents' summer home, in her descriptions to him. Of course, she would not say so in front of its elegant new owner, but on the drive home she would make it clear that the point of the cottage was its shabby simplicity, which had been all but erased except for the old clothesline stretched between two trees in the side yard, where Jacqueline had hung her Scandia linen sheets.

After they'd chatted and finished their snack, Bob wanted to take Ethan down to the dock. When Helen hesitated, then said she thought she'd rather not today, he seemed to understand finally that however generous his intentions, this visit had been a mistake. What she saw in his eyes at that moment—disappointment in his own failure to guess what might be meaningful to his wife—she felt a flash of hatred for herself and wanted to tell him, *Never mind, let's all go down*, but he'd already turned to lead Ethan out, and she was left alone with Jacqueline, before whom Helen suddenly did not wish to appear a fool.

Jacqueline seemed to discern the nature of what had passed between her guests. She asked how long they'd been married, and Helen said eight years. Jacqueline smiled, though it was not clear to Helen why. "How about you?" Helen asked. "I remember my mother saying the new owner was a widow."

"Technically, that's true." Jacqueline put on water for tea, then took out two cups and saucers without asking Helen if she wanted any. "Technically, we were married until he died, so that was twenty-four years."

Helen could tell that the other woman was waiting to be urged to elaborate. It was not in Helen's nature to do so, but she was curious, and it appeared that Jacqueline was more than willing to answer. "'Technically'?" Helen said. *That's not being nosy*, she thought. *That's just repeating her own word.*

Jacqueline brought the tea to the table and sat down across from her. "When he was in the hospital after the first heart attack, I found out he had a whole other family. Another woman, who had a child he was the father of. Not really a child—she was twelve years old. They came to see him when they thought we wouldn't be there. Why wouldn't we be there? He was my husband; he had a heart attack." She stirred sugar into her tea without making a move to drink it. Helen lifted her own cup to her mouth, knowing the question had just been rhetorical; she was expected to listen, not to speak.

"Would I ever have imagined such a thing possible? The answer is no. Not of my husband, not in a million years." Now the smile Jacqueline gave was one of self-mockery, Helen saw. "Yet there was his other daughter, crying outside the hospital room over her father the same as my daughter. Or I should say *their* father. And *our* daughter." She gave a bitter laugh before adding, "A nurse came by and asked me if they were twins."

Helen allowed a few moments to pass, out of respect for the confidence she'd just heard, before asking, "Why are you telling me this?" It was not sympathy she felt for Jacqueline Witt, but resentment. They were complete strangers to each other. It was her birthday, for God's sake. This visit was supposed to be a gift.

"Because," Jacqueline said, "I never would have thought it could happen to *me*." The look she sent across the table caused Helen to stand, without quite planning it, and for a few seconds she had to balance herself against a sudden dizziness.

She wanted to leave, but Bob and Ethan had not returned from the dock. "I changed my mind—I think I'll go down to see the lake, after all," she said, and Jacqueline made a waving gesture as if to say she understood. She did not follow her guest out to the path.

But her husband and son were already on their way back up. When he saw her, Ethan ran ahead of his father to exclaim to Helen, "I made a rock skip three times on top of the water! Dad showed me how."

"Let's go," Helen told Bob, heading him off on his way back to the cottage.

"But I want to thank her. Say good-bye."

"I already did. Really—I think she wants to be alone."

He allowed her to convince him, and they walked back to the car, Helen trying to shake off the feeling that they were being watched through the window. For the first few minutes, driving over the bumps that made up Beaver Shores Road, Ethan was the only one who spoke. He wanted to find a place near their own house to skip stones, he said. He wanted to see if he could ever make one skip ten times in a row.

When they reached the intersection, he pointed left and said, "What happens if you go that way?" and Helen turned to give him a smile filled with affection, the specific source of which—the echo she heard, in his question, of her own as a child— he could not have guessed.

"I don't know," she told Ethan. "But I always wanted to find out."

And oh, that would have been the *perfect* present! If her husband had heard the note of wishfulness in her voice, given them both a smile as if he'd had the idea up his sleeve all along, and turned the car in the direction away from the one that would lead them home.

But no. The visit had taken longer than he'd expected, Bob said; he had to get back to the house for a scheduled phone call. He was sorry if his gift hadn't turned out the way he hoped—sorry if Helen was disappointed.

Helen assured him vigorously that she wasn't. Then she asked him, "Was all that real? I mean the art, the scarf, that woman—it seemed unreal to me. Like a mirage or something. Is that just because it was so different from how I was picturing things up here all these years?"

"I know what you mean," Bob said. It was one of the

things she loved about being married to him—the surprising comfort when he affirmed her most uncertain, peculiar thoughts. "But no, it wasn't a mirage. She was real."

Helen told him Jacqueline's story—the one about her husband having a whole other life.

"Wow," Bob said. He whistled. "If it's true, that was terrible of him. Talk about betrayal."

From the back seat Ethan said, "Why wouldn't it be true?"

Helen had wanted to ask the same thing. Bob chose his next words carefully, she could tell. "It probably *is* true. It's just that sometimes people remember things the way they need to remember them, instead of the way they really happened."

Ethan said, "That doesn't make any sense."

Irritated, Helen told Bob, "I agree with him. There's no reason for you to think that woman was deluded. Or misremembering, or making anything up."

"I didn't say she was. I only said that sometimes people *do*." When Bob tapped the wheel for emphasis, she could tell *he* was irritated. "You're the one who brought it up, aren't you? You're the one who asked if she even existed."

Just to remind herself that Jacqueline had not been an illusion, in the following years Helen drove up a few times to see the cabin. The *Witt's End* sign was always there, though she never actually caught sight of Jacqueline herself again. The last time was just before Bob's arrest, which made it more than twenty-five years between that day and the warm spring morning after her son's death, when she was tempted to make the spontaneous trip north. When she realized how long it had been, she decided not to risk seeing what the place might look like now—who knew whether the cabin was even still standing?—and went to the book group at the library instead.

It turned out she had read the wrong book for that day's session, and for a short time this upset her, because she'd wanted someone to explain to her the story about the Russian housewife who carried on profound conversations with her sugar bowl. Helen didn't trust herself to understand the story, although she suspected that it was all a metaphor, that the sugar bowl was only "saying" what the housewife wanted it to say. Still, she had looked at her own sugar bowl differently—with more than a little wistfulness—ever since finishing the book.

But then she realized it would be fine with her (a relief, in fact, because sometimes these sessions seemed a little competitive to her) to just sit and listen to other people talk. The novel up for discussion was Émile Zola's *L'Assommoir*. Probably because it was such a beautiful day, there were fewer people present than usual. Helen counted eleven, including herself. Most of them she'd seen here before, but after the lecture, when Enid asked people what their "takeaway" had been from reading the novel, a newcomer at the other end of the room raised her hand and said, "I thought it was incredibly depressing. She has two goals in life: not to be beaten, and to die in her own bed. In the end, she doesn't get either of those things. What's the point of reading a book like that?" Though the woman's words might have suggested she felt duped or angry, her tone sounded more as if she really wanted Enid to explain why she had assigned them all such a miserable experience.

Next to her, Helen felt Liane jerk a little in her seat before she reached out to put a hand on Helen's knee. Puzzled, she was about to whisper, "What?" when she realized that the woman who'd asked the question was the mother of Julie Coyle. Liane's sudden movement had drawn Rae Coyle's attention to the row of seats behind her, and Helen sensed herself being recognized even as she was still feeling the shock of recognizing Rae.

It was not the first time they'd seen each other since that day in court all those years ago. But those other times were all from a distance—at the town's Fourth of July parade, in line at the post office, across Harrah's Bistro on a Saturday night. Once, they'd even attended the same Columbus Day dress sale at The Blue Flamingo, though they kept on opposite sides of the store. In every case, they each pretended not to notice the other. It was too late for that now.

Other people had taken note of the look exchanged between them, but Enid Burkhard was absorbed instead by the literary question at hand, and she was so commanding a figure to members of the group that when she went to answer it, the attention in the room swung back to her. "Zola said once"—she glanced down at her notes—"'All I care about is life, struggle, intensity.' Well?" She spread out her hands and shrugged. "Isn't that what we get in this book?" She was inviting everyone else to respond to what Rae had said.

With a measure of animation Helen could tell was aimed at impressing Enid, Liane raised her hand and said, "It was *so* real, it was almost too much. I honestly thought I wouldn't be able to stand it when the undertaker carries her out at the end and he says to her"—she flipped to the last page in her book, so she could quote the exact words—"'*There, there, you're all right now. Night-night, my lovely!*'"

Helen rose on legs she barely felt and let them propel her stiffly through the doors of the library's conference room and into the lobby, where she lowered herself onto a cushioned bench. If she'd stood up again and taken a few steps down the corridor, she would have seen the chart on the wall marking the progress of all the children enrolled in the Reading Rodeo, which she herself had been involved in organizing when Ethan was in first grade. For every book a kid read during the school year that wasn't assigned for a class, a cardboard horse designated with his or her name was advanced a certain distance around the track, and there was a prize for reaching the finish line—usually, a gift certificate donated by The Paperback Rack, which sold "gently read" and "previously enjoyed" books. The Rodeo was always careful to emphasize that it wasn't a race or any other kind of competition, but the kids didn't see it that way. Ethan won more times than not, which embarrassed Helen. It also embarrassed her that he wanted to participate in the Rodeo as long as he did, through junior high, long past the age when his classmates had dropped out. Helen knew she couldn't say anything, because what was she supposed to do, discourage her son from wanting to read? She was relieved when he said, the summer before entering high school, that maybe it was time to hang the Rodeo up.

As far as Helen knew, his favorite book had always been *Of Mice and Men*. He even wrote about it for his college application essay: "People don't stop to think about how destructive it can be to mistake the intentions of someone who is actually innocent." He went on to write about his father's experience—how he had been imprisoned for something he didn't do (although Ethan avoided specifying what the conviction was for)—and how he'd learned from this that it was crucial to dig as deeply as possible, in any given situation, to ensure "a judgment based on fact instead of fancy." Helen had tried to get him to change that last phrase, because to her it sounded like a cliché. (She also wasn't crazy about his essay topic in the first place, though Bob didn't seem to mind, which impressed her.)

After Ethan sent off those applications, the subject of his father's imprisonment had never come up in conversation among any of them until Ethan lay dying in the hospital bed.

"*Night-night, my lovely!*" A sock to the gut, recalling. The nurse had let them all sit in the room with him for a half hour after the death had been declared, before coming in to close the curtain around the bed, her tacit signal that it was time for them to go. Helen had not expected to survive leaving her son behind in the room, knowing she would never see him again. In the library lobby, she closed her eyes and leaned her head back against the wall. Not even a full minute passed before the door from the conference room opened and Rae Coyle joined her in the hall.

"Are you okay?" Rae said.

"I'm fine," Helen told her, laughing almost out loud at the wrongness of the word for what she was. The question, coming from this woman of all people, had surprised her. At the last moment she turned it into a choked swallow, giving herself a dramatic thump-slap on the chest.

Rae hesitated, appearing unsure about how to interpret this gesture on Helen's part. "I heard about your son. I'm sorry," she said, adding "Ethan" in a surreptitious tone as if testing whether Helen would challenge her right to say it.

But Helen only thanked her, automatically and without gratitude. She was trying to anticipate what she might be being set up for, with Rae Coyle being so nice.

"I saw he had children." Now Rae did venture to perch herself on the edge of the bench, and Helen felt her heartbeat accelerate. "My daughter just had her first, a boy. I went down to visit them in Atlanta last month, to meet him and help her out."

"How many daughters do you have?" Helen asked, not turning to look at Rae as she spoke, directing her words instead to the air in front of her.

"Just the one." Though Rae had dared to speak Ethan's name, she seemed to understand that the conversation would not withstand her uttering Julie's. "She hasn't had an easy time of it—two divorces behind her, and she's not even married to the father yet. But I'm hoping the baby will calm her down." She bit at her finger, exclaiming as she drew a bead of blood.

Seeing this, Helen wanted to ask her "What's *wrong* with you?" and when she heard these words in her head, she remembered Bob saying "What's *wrong* with people?" whenever they saw stories on the news about a husband throwing acid in his wife's face or someone robbing an elderly woman pushing a stroller or a Goodwill worker being stuck by dirty syringes concealed in a box of donated clothes. Now that she thought about it, she didn't remember him saying it after he spent time in prison. It was as if he'd stopped wondering, or had finally gotten an answer that satisfied him.

Rae Coyle pursed her lips around the wound she had given herself. Sucking, she told Helen, "Listen. My daughter says it was all in her imagination."

"What?" Helen assumed she had not quite made out the words correctly, since the other woman had spoken them around the finger inside her mouth.

"When I was down there. A few weeks ago. I was showing her how to burp the baby, and out of nowhere she says, 'You know what, Mom, it never happened.'" Now it was Rae's turn to laugh without a trace of enjoyment in it. "I had no idea what she was talking about. It's not something we ever mentioned. In fact, I was pretty sure she had forgotten the whole thing."

As Rae spoke, Helen tried desperately to find a way to stop her, without realizing that she was doing so. But the other woman did not receive the message.

"She said Mr. Metzger—your husband—was just helping her at the water fountain. He lifted her up so she could reach it, that's all. They'd had someone come in to teach the class about 'bad touching.' That's what started the whole thing."

A squeeze to the lungs, recalling. Doing dishes at the sink, looking out through the window at the trees nodding through the black night. Bob still sitting at the table with his Sanka as Ethan, after being excused, did his long practice in the living room. It was all Helen could do to move Ethan's music to the background of her mind and listen to Bob with the front, especially as their son became proficient, then excellent, then expert at playing Beethoven, Stravinsky, Chopin. Yet she knew he concentrated better when no one was listening, so she focused on what her husband was saying instead.

He always offered to help her clean up and she always refused. She knew he knew she would refuse, but she didn't mind, because it was easier and faster to do it herself; she did the dishes and he sat with his coffee as they reconstructed their days for each other. That particular night, Bob told her that the school board had recommended hiring a group called CAPE—Child Abuse Prevention Education—to come in and talk to all the grades about sexual abuse. *Why all?* Bob asked, at a meeting of the principals, and he was told, *Because it cost the same whether they visit sixty classes or one.* Bob thought maybe it was okay for the fourth- and fifth-graders. Maybe even third. But kindergarten? First grade? "Aren't they too young?" he asked Helen. "They're still so impressionable at that age. Wouldn't it just go putting ideas in their heads?"

She always appreciated it when he asked her advice, especially about things related to his own profession. She considered his question as she rinsed a pot out, then told him no, she didn't think so. It was probably not a bad idea. Just in case one or more of the kids had an uncle or a neighbor who was up to no good; at least they'd know it wasn't their fault, know they should tell somebody.

So the joke was on her! Persuaded by his wife's words, Bob had invited the CAPE people in, and now she was being told more than thirty years later that he'd been right all along—it had put an idea in Julie Coyle's head.

"That can't be true," she said to Rae Coyle, wondering whether she'd actually spoken the words aloud or only meant to.

"What do you mean, it can't be true? I thought you'd be happy." Rae seemed to have forgotten about her bloody finger. "I mean, I admit I had my doubts when she said he hadn't done it. She hasn't been the best mentally. Trouble with relationships, all that. The classic things you see in abused kids. I thought maybe she just convinced herself it didn't happen to her, so she could believe she was normal."

She'd tucked the tops of her hands under her jeans and was sitting forward on the bench, looking down at her own scuffed loafers. "But I don't know, she said she'd been lying all those years, and she looked like she felt so guilty. I decided to believe her."

When Helen didn't respond to this, Rae continued, "I should apologize. I *am* apologizing. Wait a minute," she said, the energy in her voice swelling as a new thought appeared to dawn on her. "Are you saying you thought he did it? Oh, my God. That never occurred to me. I mean, you stayed with him. You took him back. I always assumed you never *believed* it." The expression on her face had evolved from contrition to something bordering on salacious intrigue.

Helen drew in caution on her next breath. Whatever she did, she could not betray herself, or Bob—their marriage, their family (though of course, she would realize, moments later, she'd already done so)—and let Rae Coyle know that she was right. Instead of answering, she said, "So is this just some kind of coincidence? You happen to run into me at the library and decide to—what—confess?" She made her voice sound accusatory, as if accusing the other woman, at this point, made sense.

Rae shook her head, not seeming to take the offense Helen had hoped she would. "No. My friend Maureen, the one I came with, told me she'd seen you here. I was interested in the book club anyway. I was kind of killing two birds with one stone." She appeared to regret the word *killing* the

191

moment it was out.

So you were stalking me, Helen thought but did not say. She said, "You could have written me a letter."

"I thought about it. But then I thought this would be better." Rae's shoulders shrank. "Who writes letters anymore?" She seemed to hear the combativeness in her voice, and dialed it back to concession. "I guess I was wrong."

The Literary League was letting out of the conference room, Liane leading the way. She was trying without success to contain the excited curiosity in her face about what she might find in the lobby, with Helen and Rae Coyle having both left the room. Helen saw her friend coming toward her and stood up. They had made a date to go out for coffee, but in a voice she tried to keep from shaking as she left Rae Coyle alone on the bench, she told Liane she didn't feel up to it.

That night it occurred to her that she hadn't thought to ask whether Julie Coyle might be willing to recant, officially, what she'd said all those years ago. She went so far as to look up Rae's phone number in the town directory, and to think about how she might bring up the question, but stopped short of dialing the number. Instead she called her daughter-in-law and asked Sandra to make her an appointment with the realtor in Scottsdale they'd met the day after Ethan's funeral. What changed her mind? Sandra asked, and Helen shook her head before remembering that Sandra couldn't see her. "It's just time," she said.

Days, months, even a year later—after she'd moved out to Arizona, taking a few things with her from the house but selling or leaving the bulk of it behind—she had allowed herself, mostly, to forget it all. Mostly. Fallen away were the woman fumbling peanuts down her shirt on the plane, the two doctors pulling French fries distractedly from the same paper plate, her daughter-in-law's white hair (although it had been restored, since, to the smoky brunette color Helen had always associated with Sandra, which was a relief), even the beseeching saguaro outside the hospital room. The only thing she couldn't lose, no matter how hard she tried, was the expression on her son's face when she told him she thought it was possible his father had done the inexplicable, inexcusable thing he'd been accused of.

It was not the same expression she would have seen if she had pointed a cocked gun at him or approached his face with a pillow. It was not panic or fear or dread. It was shock, pure and simple, and it was worse than any of those others would have been. Which was why, she knew, it would not leave her.

Six years passed, and she was sitting in the fifth row of bleachers at Cadence's high school commencement when she glanced up toward the observation window separating the gym from the lobby, where the overflow audience stood, and saw Bob straining for a view of his granddaughter graduating.

Bob.

It couldn't be, of course. She knew that. She looked away, to the row of seniors in their caps and gowns moving across the stage to collect their diplomas. The principal was still reading off the L's; Cadence would be in the next batch. Helen looked up to the window again expecting the figure of her imagination to have vanished, but there he was, trying without much success to press closer to the front row next to the glass. Her husband. The woman next to him said something to him about his nudging—Helen saw her lips move, an unhappy mouth—and he lifted his hand to her like a white flag of surrender before backing away, out of Helen's sight.

That was how she knew it was her husband—the raised hand saying, *Okay, You're right, I give in.* He had made the same gesture throughout their marriage, even before. He'd made it the night she told him she thought having the CAPE people in to talk to the children about "bad touching" was a good idea. He'd even made it, she remembered, the morning of the day he died, when she said she couldn't imagine anything more boring than Outcomes Assessment.

She stood and began moving to the end of the bleacher aisle. "Sorry, guys," she whispered to her daughter-in-law and Robert, both of whom looked at her as if she were out of her mind. They'd all arrived at the school three hours early to claim these seats. Sandra asked if she was okay, but Helen didn't answer. How could she, with what she might be moving toward?

Of course, by the time she reached the lobby, he was gone. She pushed through the overflow throng until she was next to the woman who'd been elbowing Bob aside. "Did you see a man trying to get in here to see better? Kind of short, kind of bald?"

"Not that I noticed," the woman said without looking at her. Someone tapped Helen on the shoulder and said, "Do you mind?"

She stepped away until she had enough room around her to take a breath.

She spotted him in the parking lot, walking toward a beat-up Rambler. It was entirely too easy to overtake him, grab his arm, and say his name. Of course, it was *not* him—not her dead husband. (What was she *thinking*?) The man she'd followed (chased?) turned his face at her touch, showing an expression she could not read (Defiance? Alarm? Pity?), as the echo of Bob's name rang in the air between them.

Confused, she saw that, in fact, he did not actually resemble her husband in some important ways; this man had long hair, long enough to stick down behind his shirt collar, and he wore the shirt untucked. These two aspects of appearance Bob would never have allowed. He fitted a key into the door lock of the Rambler. He was clumsy, palsied or hurried or both, and it took him three tries. "Not me, not me," the man muttered, shooing her; he might as well have been saying *Get away, get away.* He sped off without looking but there were no other cars leaving the lot, with the ceremony still going on inside the school. She watched the Rambler recede ahead of her in the distance, toward Camelback. Standing there between a Volvo and a Camry, she clenched and unclenched her fists at her sides in a state of paralysis both physical and psychic, until behind her she heard a firecracker explode.

That's what it sounded like, though it did not take long, after everyone had been evacuated and it was determined that the only injuries were superficial, for the first responders to ascertain that the sound was that of a bomb going off, but not in the way it might have. Before the cheers and congratulations and cap-tossing in the gym could commence, the powder in the backpack left behind by the man in the Rambler popped and fizzled beneath where he'd set it under the bleachers. Was there a timing device he activated after fleeing the building, perhaps moments before he heard Helen calling him by a name that was not his own? Or had he set it off *after* he waved her away—as he tore into the street thinking that he might witness the carnage he had caused, from his rearview mirror? Did it make him even happier than he might have felt otherwise, to look her in the face and anticipate what she and the rest of them were about to suffer?

But the suffering turned out to be minimal, because Helen had interrupted and no doubt flustered him. She was the one responsible for his being caught, when she responded to the police's plea for anyone with information to come forward. She could not tell them that she'd chased a man she'd thought was her dead husband, so she said only that she had gone out for some air and said hello to the man, then watched him get in his car and speed away just before the building blew up. When they asked for a description, she described Bob and added long hair, and they put out a sketch that looked so much like him that she had to turn away when it was flashed repeatedly on the TV. The man was arrested that same night, in the drive-through line at Filibertos.

The news reports referred to Helen as a person in the right place at the right time, because the exchange she'd had with the bomber had apparently delayed his ability to detonate just long enough to avoid the blast he'd intended. "'Hero' is more like it," her grandson declared, and it was so like something Ethan would have said that Helen had to put on a sweater against a sudden breathtaking chill. She was not a hero, but the opposite, she understood—a coward who'd pursued a phantom she hoped would absolve her of what she'd done to her husband and what she'd done to her son. Was she crazy? She wished she were crazy, so she could blame it on that.

The accused man did not deny it, but he did resist the accusations of terrorism. It was not terrorism, he explained. He'd planned the explosion because his ex-wife had not invited him to their daughter's commencement. Helen could tell, from the earnestness of the statement he made before the court, that this made sense to him. His ex-wife and daughter could have died if the bomb had done what it was supposed to do, but he had known this would happen, and it was only fair because of what they'd done to him. What about the innocent people who could have died along with them? The man shrugged. "No such thing as innocent. Everybody's got something they could be punished for."

Two years later, it was her turn. She knew it without need-ing to hear it directly from the doctors, and she did not tell Sandra and the children, who were not children anymore. At the end of October, for what she understood was the final time, she flew back East, took a hotel room near the airport, and hired a nurse's aide named Phyllis to drive her up to the lake. It had been so long, and she was taking such strong medication, that she wondered briefly if she would remember the route. But when it came time to direct Phyllis, she felt no hesitation, only a growing sense of calm she could not recall since before Ethan had been diagnosed. Actually—she realized, as Phyllis eased her car over the bumps of Beaver Shores Road—she could not remember feeling this way since long before that, before the trouble involving Bob and Julie Coyle. She gulped it in (this sensation she was tempted to call joy, even in the face of what would come soon), along with the scent of pine and the breeze on the sun-chilled water as they pulled off the road at the top of the private dirt drive. She asked Phyllis to wait for her, then got out and headed toward the cabin and the lake, which spread out on three sides in a winking silver sheen.

She halfway dreaded running into Jacqueline Witt again after all these years, but it was obvious, as she approached, that the place had been shuttered for the cold season. She might have missed Jacqueline by only a few days.

She passed the bulkhead, anticipating the anxiety she'd always felt near it, even after her grandfather put sturdy aluminum doors in place of the rotted wood ones she'd fallen through. But this time she felt no fear. Approaching the water's edge, she saw that the dock had been rebuilt, widened and lengthened to extend another ten feet into the lake. As a child—especially after she'd fallen into the cellar—she'd been afraid every time she and her mother and her grandparents were on the dock at the same time; the wood always shook a little beneath her feet when she took the first steps onto it, though her grandfather said this was just her imagination.

But these planks were solid, and she walked them to the far edge. From across the water she heard sounds she had not anticipated, voices laughing and shouting as if The Estate were hosting one of its family celebrations. They were the same sounds she had often heard during her childhood summers, but the pitch of high cheer seemed out of place for after Labor Day.

Was this only her imagination, too? She cupped her ear and turned it to better hear the noise. "Ready or not, here I come!" a teenager shouted, and then Helen heard the splash of someone landing in the lake.

No, it couldn't be. This was October. Besides, that girl would be the same age as Helen now, probably a grandmother herself.

Why had she never managed to persuade her mother to drive around the lake? Why hadn't she driven *herself* there when she was in her own car and it was her own decision?

Of course she wanted to know what was over there—of course she did. But maybe, she saw now, this wasn't as true as she'd always thought it was. Maybe she was more afraid than she was curious about what lay on the other side.

Well, better late than never. When she returned to the car, she would have Phyllis drive back to the top of Beaver Shores Road, and ask her to turn left instead of right. What was there to be afraid of now? Nothing that could come from another human being, she understand that for sure.

Despite the chill in the air she sat down on the dock, took her shoes and socks off, and dunked her feet. The water's coldness shocked and gratified her, and she wondered how many generations of minnows had spawned between the ones she watched shoot away from her when she was a child disrupting their habitat with her kicks, and the ones that dispersed now from her intruding feet. "Too yucky," she'd always called to her grandfather when he tried to entice her into actually standing on the bottom. Almost smiling, she whispered, "too yucky" now, toward the depths.

"And he always said, 'How can you be so sure without

coming in to see for yourself?'"

She spun around so fast she knocked her foot on the dock post, but didn't have time to notice the pain through her alarm. *Bob.* He was standing at the head of the dock, smiling across at her. She leapt up and exclaimed, realizing how stupid she'd been to leave Phyllis behind—to come alone down here where no one could help her if she ran into trouble.

It wasn't really him, of course. She knew that, after the first moment, even though she saw him standing right there in front of her, dressed in work slacks and a button-down shirt, and the tie she'd given him on the birthday before he died—red diamonds scattered on a bright blue background. It had been a dare of sorts, and he never wore it when he was alive. He'd never been a man comfortable in bold colors. But the tie looked good on him, as she had known it would.

"It's you who believes in ghosts, right?" he asked. "Not me. Not me."

"You're not real," she whispered, more to herself than to him. Without knowing she was going to, she gave a strangled laugh and added, "You're the sugar bowl."

The apparition laughed back. "You know what I am." It was his natural way as a teacher to avoid answering a question directly. He'd told Helen once that most of the time, people already possessed the answers they wanted; they just needed to be led to what they already knew. He stretched his arms toward the sky, a gesture she'd never seen in him and one that touched her unexpectedly.

But everything about this encounter was unexpected, wasn't it? And could it be called an *encounter* when you were really just inventing the other person in your mind—when it was a hallucinatory side effect of the powerful medication you could not do without?

Her head buzzed from the dissonance of understanding

199

this at the same time she was speaking aloud to him, as if they were two people standing twelve feet apart from each other after a separation of nearly twenty years, not to mention the further separation that divides the living from the dead.

She had two choices: continue the conversation, or walk away. Walking away would be saner, and safer, but what difference did that make now?

"I wish you *were* real." She took a step closer, even though she was afraid it would make him disappear. "There are so many things I wish I could say to you."

He shrugged and smiled, a combination of movements she remembered all too well; it had always struck her as inviting and dismissive at the same time. "So say them."

"But what's the point? I'd only be talking to myself. It's not as if I can actually apologize to the real—you." She laughed, feeling flushed. Another symptom, or a side effect that hadn't appeared before now? "It's too late."

"You have nothing to apologize for." The real Bob would have moved toward her then, to reinforce how much he meant it. The conjured one stayed where he was.

"Yes, I do. Of course I do. I found out from Rae Coyle . . . the truth." Helen faltered, coughing slightly on the old name she hadn't spoken in years. "But you must already know that. Right? You know about Ethan, and you know I thought you might have—" But even though there was so little left to lose, she failed to finish what she'd set out to say.

"Yes. I know." Now he did take a step closer, and she blushed from shame.

"They said kids didn't make up things like that!" She covered her face with her hands, then yanked them away so she could focus on accusing herself. "But how could I have believed anything more than what *you* told me?"

He'd come near enough to touch her, and she willed him to reach out so that she'd be convinced beyond measure of how false this all was. But his phantom hands remained alongside his phantom sides.

"Yes," he murmured. "How could you?"

The world wavered in front of her. *I'm going to faint now*, she thought. *Please, let me faint.* But then he reached out to support her. She could feel his hand on her elbow. How was that possible, when she knew he didn't really exist?

"I always thought we would talk about it," she told him. "Someday, during all that time after you came back home. But I didn't know how to say anything, and you never brought it up." She paused to lick her lips, the gesture she'd heard cats make when they feel like puking. "I took your not bringing it up as a sign of—something."

Did he smile, hearing this? No, the opposite. "I didn't think I had to," he said, and he'd never sounded so sad.

Of course she had misread what was on her husband's face. If she'd been able to read him correctly, none of this would have happened.

"Did you think," he went on, "that because I seemed content to go to conferences about things like Outcomes Assessments, that because I was so *boring*, I must have some secret life? Some hidden excitement I couldn't share with you or anyone else, like the excitement of touching a child?"

Until she heard it, she hadn't identified this thought to herself, though now she understood that it had always lodged itself just below her own reach. Why did he have access to it, when she had not?

Because, she reminded herself, he *is* that part of your mind. It was almost enough to make her smile.

"Well, it turns out the joke's on you, Hel—I really *am* that boring!"

She let all her muscles go slack and waited to collapse on the dock, but he wouldn't let her. "You know what did excite me? I liked going to work in the morning, and I liked coming home at the end of the day. I liked sitting there with my Sanka after supper, while Ethan was practicing, when we talked. Did you ever realize that after I came back from Fishkill, we never did that anymore?"

No, she didn't think she'd realized this. Things had just been one way before, and then they were another.

"I loved you," he said. "*Love* you. Present tense."

"I loved you, too." She hurried to correct herself. "I mean, *love*."

His expression told her that he knew better. "You can't really call it love, though, can you? What you felt, after Julie Coyle." Saying the girl's name took something out of him, whether he was real or not; she could see this. "It wasn't her fault," he added. "She was so young. She was confused."

Even as she felt overwhelmed by febrility, Helen remembered that she'd always admired this about her husband: the way he refused to think the worst about anyone until it had been proven to him.

"But she ruined your life." She had to lick her lips again before she could continue. "*Our* lives. Ethan's."

"No," her husband said. "You did that."

The words struck her chest like a shove. "I did that," she whispered. "You're right. It was me."

When he didn't respond, she considered it a mercy. "And Ethan," she said, their son's name a cry in her throat. "The last thing I said to him—when instead I could have told him you weren't capable of such a thing—" She waited, praying for Bob to punish her for it. But he did not.

A haze moved slowly toward her from the horizon. Or was she seeing something else that wasn't there?

She summoned everything inside her to form the question it had all been leading up to—not just these moments on the dock, but for more years than she cared to count. She could tell that Bob was waiting, curious not about the question itself but about whether she had the courage to ask it.

"If a person regrets something she's done, but there's nobody left to remember, does it *matter* that she did it? Or does it all get erased as if it didn't happen?" The desperation in her voice was evident to them both, she knew. "Or say she also did some good things, things that could even be called—heroic. Does it all even out?"

He was on the other side of her now, speaking from inside the lake. "You know the answer to that as well as I do." He held out a hand. "You know it *better.*" She took the hand as she stepped down to join him in the water. It was warm now, not cold, but she felt no surprise.

"There's a stone in here somewhere with your name on it," he reminded her. "Somewhere on the bottom."

She told him she was afraid as he drew her deeper, though she wasn't sure it was true.

"You'll get over it," he said, and then he smiled.

"Wait!" Helen whispered. "I'm not ready. I need—"

But Bob had vanished. A saguaro stood in his place, its arms stretched out wide above the water. The flimsy door buckled beneath Helen, and she began to fall.

"*It's me. You're all right now.*" She deserved no comfort, yet comfort was there. "*Night-night, my lovely!*" He reappeared to catch her right before she would have hit bottom, and finally carried her across to the other side.

INFINITE DIMENSIONS

Start

It began with mazes, simple ones, when the boy was three. The man was not his father, but he was usually assumed to be when the two of them were out together in the world. At three, the boy used a crayon—pink, usually—to mark a shaky line through the fat tubes and arteries the man had drawn for him. At that time the maze entrances were designated by a smiling bear wearing a pink bow tie, who held a sign saying, *Welcome!* At the destinations, the signs declared, *You did it!* By the time the boy was six, the bear had been retired, and the mazes lay without illustration between the letters *S* and *F*. They grew more and more challenging, to the point that the man was forced to consult a puzzle resource for advice. Each time the boy found his way through—he used a mechanical pencil now, though it was rare that he needed to erase—he asked for a harder one next time.

The man and his wife, who was a friend of the boy's mother, took care of the boy after school on Wednesdays. The once-a-week arrangement suited them all. The man told his clients he was not available on Wednesday afternoons; his wife, a professor, scheduled her classes at other times. The boy's mother, who was raising her son alone and who did not have any family around, felt grateful for the extra love the boy received. For it was not merely a babysitting arrangement; though originally it had been the wife who felt most invested in spending time with the boy, both she and her husband grew more devoted to him than either had expected.

On the other days of the week, the boy went to an after-school program run by the gym teacher and the librarian, with each session consisting of dodge ball games followed by individual reading time, which at some point devolved into nap time for most of the kids. Not so the boy. In first grade he was already reading books that had been ordered for the third grade class. As he read them, he rubbed the red spots on his face where the ball had hit before he could dodge it. The rubs appeared to be aimed at relieving or soothing the sting of a rubber smack.

At some point, it was inevitable that the boy would understand he had been targeted and aimed at, not merely standing in the wrong place when the ball came fast and hard across the line dividing the teams. He brought it up with the maze-maker's wife. "It very hurted," he said, and the woman kissed the top of his head and told him she was sorry. Her husband overheard their exchange, but he didn't say anything about it. Instead he invited the boy to try his new maze, which had taken the man the better part of a morning to construct. The boy began working it in his usual way, his blond head bent so close over the paper that his nose almost touched. It took him long enough that they had to delay supper, but not as long as the man had anticipated it would.

"I hope you're proud of yourself," he said after the boy laid the pencil down.

"I am." The boy sounded surprised, as if he had heard of the concept of pride but never quite felt it until now. "Please make it harder next time," he added, and the man promised he would.

When he was eight, the boy graduated from mazes to math, which the man said was really the same thing in a different form. Mathematics had been the foundation of what the man did for a living, though he had never shared much of it with his wife. He'd never really shared it with anyone until the boy appeared in his life and began asking for problems to solve.

The maze-maker's wife died when the boy was ten, after an illness that had forced them to suspend their regular visits. At her funeral, the boy went to stand before the man as he greeted the guests. His mother said, "What are you doing? Come back here, come with me," but when the boy shook his head, the man asked her if it would be all right for her son to remain where he was. As he asked, he gripped the shoulders of the boy's sweater, and appeared even to be held up, in a way, by the small body before him. In this manner, the two of them received condolences until there was no one left in the line.

The following week, the man picked the boy up from school, as his wife had always done, and took him to a chess club for a lesson. At first the boy balked, saying he preferred to learn from the man himself, but the man said to trust him; as soon as the boy learned what he needed to know, they could forgo the lessons and settle into playing the game together.

It didn't take long. Within a few months, their routine for Wednesday afternoons was set: first math, then chess, then dinner, after which the man drove him home. When they talked, it was seldom about school, or other children the boy's age; often it was about the man's wife.

"You guys never had any kids," the boy said once, both a statement and a question.

"That's right."

"Was that because you didn't want them?"

"No. That wasn't it." The man put his fork down, and the boy's expression showed that he was waiting. "It very hurted," the man said, which was both an answer and not. They smiled at each other, then looked down at their plates.

Another time, when they were playing chess, the boy said,

206

"Have you ever noticed that most people don't really listen to what other people are saying?" He was contemplating what his best move might be when it came his turn. "Have you noticed they're not even listening to *themselves?*"

"Yes," the man said, reaching for his queen. "I have noticed that."

In junior high school, the boy won a regional mathematics competition; in high school he won a national one, along with a scholarship to a university more than half the country away. The boy (who was not, of course, a boy anymore) accepted the scholarship when the man encouraged him to, even though he said he was nervous about going so far away. They remained in touch by email, and played ongoing games of virtual chess; often when the boy came home for breaks, they met to play in person. He chose calculus as his major, and graduated with honors before moving on to study for his advanced degrees. In another five years he went on the job market and was hired as an assistant professor of mathematics at a branch of the public university system in his home state, close to where he had grown up.

By this time, the man was close to retiring from his own job. When he decided to marry again, he and the new woman invited the boy and his mother to dinner one night, so they could all get acquainted. To the boy's surprise, the man pulled out a folder in which he had kept the mazes and math work they'd done together, beginning with that first pink-crayoned route between the two drawings of the bear in a bow tie.

"That is adorable," the new woman said. The man asked the boy to talk about his research, and the rest of them heard about something called the Hilbert Space Method, which extends the methods of vector algebra and calculus from two- and three-dimensional spaces to those occupying any finite or infinite number of dimensions. His mother said it was all beyond her, she had a different kind of brain entirely and didn't know where her son's had come from, and the man asked what kind of problem the Hilbert Space Method might be applied to. Well, the boy said, it could be used to analyze and predict the movement of a stretched wire, like that on a stringed musical instrument or a taut rubber band.

The boy's mother poured herself some more wine. "My question is, why would you *want* to predict the movement of a stretched wire?" she asked, and the boy said it wasn't a practical application, it was all very abstract, laypeople weren't supposed to understand it.

"You did a good job of explaining," the man said. "I think I have the gist." The woman he was going to marry said that the kind of work she did was pretty abstract, too, and it could be frustrating when people didn't necessarily get why you were doing it.

When the boy's own children were old enough, he tried to teach them about mazes, but neither of them showed any interest or aptitude. He failed to be granted tenure at the university, because—he was told—there was not enough demand for the type of mathematics he specialized in. It was too narrow, the reviewers said. Not enough students were going into the field.

He responded with a letter protesting their decision. *That would seem all the more reason to support this work*, he wrote. *Otherwise, there is no telling what might be lost.*

But his appeal was futile. After he left the job, he could not find anyone else to hire him to teach what he himself loved but had been deemed obsolete. A long period followed during which he seemed to have lost his way at every turn, both in his profession and his personal life. Fifteen years after the dinner with the man and the woman who would become his second wife, the boy—who was now the age the man had been when their lives intersected for the first time—found himself sitting alone in the shadows of a house nobody except he lived in anymore. After a few hours without moving from the seat he'd sunk into, he roused himself to walk around the living room, pausing to touch the objects he'd laid on a table: his daughter's old jump rope, a half-filled bottle of pills with a faded label, a pen on a piece of paper. It was the pen his hand lingered on. He picked it up and set it down again. Then he resumed his seat.

He sat that way all through the night. When the sun came up, he moved to the window as if to pull the curtains against the light, then paused in the action and went instead to the desk in a corner of the room. Reaching it, he bent to blow a film of dust from its surface. He opened a top drawer, removing the folder the man had shown him at dinner that night, which the second wife had given him at the man's funeral. It had not been opened since that day; in fact, the boy had shoved it into the drawer so hastily, as if to get it out of his sight as soon as possible, that the papers inside were askew as he pulled them out now.

He neatened the stack and began to study the pages one by one. At times a look of pain crossed his face and he rubbed it; at other times, he appeared to smile. Some of his own long-ago solutions he traced with a finger. He moved them closer to the light.

The man had arranged them in order, from the first and easiest on top (The bear! That bow tie!) to the most difficult equation on the bottom, the one the boy had had to take home with him, because he couldn't finish in time, the night of his last visit to the two of them before the man's wife got too sick.

But wait. That was *not* the final problem in the pile: beneath it lay a maze the boy had never seen before. Rather than having been hand-drawn like all the others, it appeared to have been devised on a computer. As with all of them, the man had signed his initials in a corner. But this puzzle he had, in addition, inscribed to the boy. After the boy's name he'd written, *If you can solve this, you can solve anything.*

He sat looking at the page for many minutes, during which he barely blinked. The sun was fully risen by now, though no one else in his neighborhood appeared to be awake. He opened another drawer and found, without needing to rummage, his old pencil. Then he lowered his head and began the distant but familiar search for the way out.

Finish

ACKNOWLEDGMENTS

Many thanks to the editors of the journals in which these stories appeared in somewhat different form: "Kwashiorkor" in *Colorado Review*; "Original Work" in *Shenandoah*; "Providence" in *Fifth Wednesday*; "Cliff Walk" and "Ghost Story" in *Great Jones Street*; "Bequest" and "Sky Harbor" in *Ascent*; "Divertimento" in *Pangyrus*; "Infinite Dimensions" in *The Florida Review*.

For their contributions I'm indebted to Jennifer Ankner-Edelstein, Colin Dockrill, Karen Feldscher, Katie Gergel, August Henry, Philip Holland, Samuel Holland, Dan Johnson, Larisa Levich, Lori Milken, Jessica Mileo, Joseph Olshan, Lauren Richman, Adam Schwartz, Ann Treadway, and Kimberly Witherspoon.

Grateful acknowledgment and admiration to Katherine Anne Porter for her story "The Grave," from which I took inspiration and borrowed language, a character's name, and, I hope, her spirit.

Finally, my continuing appreciation to the teams at Inkwell and Delphinium, and to the administration at Emerson College, for their sustaining and generous support of my work.

ABOUT THE AUTHOR

Jessica Treadway is the Flannery O'Connor Award–winning author of the story collections *Please Come Back to Me* and *Absent Without Leave* , and the novels *The Gretchen Question*, *And Give You Peace*, *Lacy Eye* and *How Will I Know You?* She is a native of Albany, New York, and currently lives in Massachusetts, where she is a Senior Distinguished Writer in Residence at Emerson College in Boston.